The Thriving Of Willows

Emma Pate,
Enjoy this Read,
Karry Moser

Karri L. Moser

This novel is dedicated to Jake--strength, perseverance, resilience, truth, and standing firm when faced with any challenges—always. I am awed by your creative sparks and artful soul. Keep sharing your words. You inspire me to keep sharing mine.

"When life gets to be too heavy, tread lightly and bend like the willow tree, so that you too, do not break"

Ja-Nae Duane

ISBN 9781730924545

Printed in the U.S.A.

First Edition

Forward

The Thriving of Willows, the sequel to Moose Pond Lodge, arose out of a need to tell more about these characters and a desire to write more about nature—especially willow trees. These trees, in my mind, look hypnotically graceful and protective. Their branches reach down, surround everything in their path and provide a shield, a canopy. Within this graceful, wispy exterior is an unspoken strength. Willow trees have the unique ability to bend, sway, and take almost anything nature can throw their way without breaking. Their strong, complicated roots reach far below the earth and search for vital nutrients without losing that delicate exterior. The bark of the willow has also been used for thousands of years to alleviate all kinds of pain. Willows are no different than most women. Women thrive against the odds, weather unfathomable storms, and use their graceful talents to shield and heal the ones they love. Each woman in The Thriving of Willows takes on a storm and perseveres when others may have given up, may have broken, or withered away. They bend, adjust with the wind, and remain standing despite what threatens to overtake them or break the bonds with those they love. They each come out on the other side of this storm stronger, wiser, and even more resilient than when the storm clouds first swirled above. While not perfect, not flawless, and not always right, each of the three women—Molly, Allie, and Simone--thrive once the sun comes out again.

Introduction

April 8th

Allie

Even though Allie was supposed to get some rest, it was Saturday. She never missed a Saturday once the snow melted. It was her only time to sit in the Public Garden, breathe in air mixed with earth, not concrete, and take pictures of the weeping willows. She'd take shot after shot of the branches tickling the few blades of grass that optimistically defied predictions of another snow day. She admired their tenacity, their will to survive. Allie hoped to absorb some of that will as she took a seat and drew up her legs. She usually sprawled out her lean body, staked her claim in the park, but not today. Today Allie wanted to make herself as small as she felt. Maybe, she thought, if she could ball herself up enough she wouldn't feel so empty, so gutted. Her eyes followed one of the longest willow branches to the point where it met the thick, sturdy trunk of the tree. Allie wondered if that branch snapped, tumbled to the ground below and turned to dust in an instant, would the rest of the tree notice? Would that willow go on growing, swaying, tickling the new grass below never knowing a piece of it was gone forever? Or, would it scream in pain and stretch out its surviving branches to instinctively grab onto something that was no longer there?

Allie kicked off her shoes and curled her feet around the edge of the bench. She wrapped her long arms around her legs and clasped them at her shins. She still had slight cramping but nothing like she felt Thursday after dinner. Allie's phone buzzed next to her. Jonah's smiling face graced the screen. She ignored it. Then, ignored it again. When she called him Thursday night, the word 'miscarriage' made it to the tip of her tongue. But, her lips pursed shut, and she swallowed it back down into the pit of her stomach. Instead of trying again, she let Jonah talk. He said he had finalized his vacation days so that they could return to Moose Pond Lodge for their first anniversary in July. He was loving the Chicago skyline and, of course, the pizza. He had already texted her a dozen pictures from three pizza shops within walking distance of his hotel. But, he missed her and couldn't wait until the month was over. Work was work. She let his words fill the space inside her.

As he spoke that night, Allie decided she couldn't tell him over the phone. It could wait three weeks. She didn't even know they were pregnant until she felt a violent stabbing as she cleared her plate. She could wait twenty-one days to tell him what they lost, what they never knew they had. After Allie swiped "ignore" for the third time since she got to the park, she bit her lip and clasped her hands tighter around her shins.

Allie released her long legs and let them fall to the ground below. She exhaled until every ounce of air escaped her thin, tired body. She drew in breath and reached her camera. The sun was peeking through, and if Allie got up, wandered to the other side of the tree or peeked under that protective canopy, she could get the perfect shot. Maybe, she thought, a perfect shot would fill the hollowness in her. Photographing nature, especially the willows in the Public Garden, always had before.

April 8th

Simone

Simone tied the belt of her pink cashmere cardigan. Angel had always loved her in pink. She glanced around at an ocean of faces floating by as she stood planted in their favorite spot in Central Park, New York City. Simone hoped no one who knew her was in the city that afternoon. She tapped the tip of each finger to her thumbs, one by one, in unison as she scanned the crowd of tourists. Simone wasn't sure she'd recognize him after 20 years. She squinted as her eyes caught sight of a tall, dark-skinned man with a multi-colored beanie on his head. He was looking down as he descended the stone steps. His hands were in his jean pockets. Simone gasped when he looked up. It was Angel. He was a little gray, but there was no doubt it was him. She re-tied her belt and swooped her stringy red hair behind her ears. *Was it too late to run?* She thought. *Had he seen me?* If she ran now, she could crouch underneath the secluded canopy of a willow tree, and her life would remain as it had the last two decades. It would stay near-perfect, clean, tidy. He would remain a memory she let bubble to the surface in between sleep and awake, or on days she was infinitely bored with her charity work or historical society duties. He would simply stay in her mind as part of that one year away from reality, that period the family quietly called her 'breakdown.'

She jerked her head to the right, then the left. She tapped her foot, gearing herself up for a sprint to the other side of the fountain and off behind the trees. Then, she looked his way again. Their eyes locked. Her foot stopped, and she relaxed her hands for the first time in what felt like forever. There was nowhere to go. There was nowhere she wanted to go. Simone dropped her shoulders and let her head fall to the side. Angel reached her and wrapped his arms around her before she could utter a word. Simone collapsed into him and cried. All fear of being seen with him melted away. He was all that mattered once again. He caressed her hair and whispered in her ear like he always had before. "Shhh. I'm here, Mona. I'm here now."

Everything she felt during that year so long ago exploded and raced through her body as he held her tighter. It wasn't gone. It wasn't a dream, a phase, or a 'breakdown.' She was awake now. He pulled back enough to look in her eyes. His hand slid to her side and rested on the very spot where his name had been inked in cursive. Simone felt an ache in her heart at the thought of telling him it was erased, laser removed. Her family spent so much time and money trying to erase any trace of him after that year. As she stood in front of him next to Bethesda Fountain on a spring day, she realized they had erased nothing. They had merely covered him up.

"This can't—" she said.

"I know. I know. But for right now, this afternoon, let's just pretend it can. You know, like we did that year." Angel said.

He leaned in and kissed her. His lips were still the softest she'd ever known. His warmth melted everything that was cold inside of her. Simone felt dizzy. She pulled back. She steadied herself, closed her eyes and leaned her forehead into his. "Just this afternoon, Angel. Nothing more." As he stood in front of her, Simone knew she was lying to him and herself. It was already something more.

His hand slipped into hers. He led her through the crowd. *I remember this feeling*, she thought. Bliss. It's pure bliss.

April 8th

Molly

The dampness of the morning didn't stop Molly from opening the attic window. She rarely went into that attic since taking over Moose Pond Lodge a year earlier. But, today was different. It was her birthday. From the time she was a kid, she'd climb through the attic window and scoot out onto the roof. The shingles would scratch her hands sometimes. Her mother hated it and would stand in the driveway of the main lodge building yelling at her to get back inside, especially if it was raining, which was common the first week of April in Maine. Her father would cheer her on.

"The world is yours, Molly! Shout out your wishes! Shout it to the world." He'd say from behind her nervous mother. Molly would giggle as her mom would scold her dad. Then, she'd slowly stand and steady her tiny legs on the roof, far back from the edge. She'd cup her hands, throw her head back and shout her wishes into the sky, believing someone was up there listening.

It was her first birthday in Maine in almost 20 years since she left after high school. No one was waiting below to encourage her ritual or warn her of the dangers. Both her mother and father were gone. Molly stood and retied short her blonde hair into a tiny ponytail sprouting from the top of her head. Strands were blowing in her eyes as the wind picked up. A storm was coming. She could tell by how the willow branches swayed below. She pulled the sleeves of her worn-out sweatshirt over her hands and drew them up to her face.

"I wish for this season be more successful than last year!" she shouted.

"I wish for Emerson to stay healthy and safe!"

"I wish to keep everything exactly as it is!" She laughed. "God don't let anything change. Let's just keep life exactly like this. No surprises!" She instantly realized the absurdity of not wanting anything new, different, or exciting to unfold as a birthday wish. She laughed a little to herself. But since last summer and since giving Zack another chance, she liked the simplicity of her life, the casualness of what they had together. Molly jumped in too fast and fierce last summer. She made Zack promise he could come back into her life if they kept it light, love in moderation.

Molly let her arms fall to her side as she drew in a deep breath. She sat down and crossed her legs. Meditating was her latest ritual as she sought to keep her sense of balance. Her thoughts immediately went to Zack. He was coming over tonight with dinner and a cake. She had let him back in her life, but only on the surface. She couldn't give him more without getting too close to the edge again. Losing him once sent her into a tailspin. She didn't trust herself to remain steady and sober if she lost him again. She thought meditating might help her find a way to keep an avalanche of feelings at bay. As if somehow, meditating could create a protective shield around her, like the weeping willows did when she'd hide and have picnics alone in the clearing. It hadn't. It simply made her knees ache. She was happy and satisfied with how things were at this moment in every aspect of her life. *Why mess up a good thing?* Molly thought. Keeping him at arm's length was working for her. Surely, she could make it work for him. Her wish to keep everything the same made sense. Letting Zack stay the night while Emerson was home and referring to themselves as a couple to guests and people in town had to be enough for him. It was enough for her. All things in moderation, she told herself. Molly knew that was the key. She couldn't get rattled, thrown off balance again. She needed to stay in control of herself and what they had together. She needed it to remain exactly as it was. It was manageable. There was no need or desire for growth or change.

A strong gust of wind whipped across her face. She knew it was time to crawl back inside the attic window for protection. There was nothing moderate or manageable about the storm that was coming. She wasn't about to get trapped in the middle of it. Avoiding storms was becoming her second nature.

The Thriving of Willows

Chapter 1

Allie

Allie unfolded a paper bag containing a sandwich made the night before. She squinted as she slid her sunglasses from her face. The July sun was blinding. As she laid them by her side on the bench, the wind picked up and blew her black hair across her eyes. The branches of the towering weeping willows swayed back and forth, as they did every weekend she made her way to her bench. Allie basked in each second of being in the Public Garden, the heart of the city and first botanical garden in the country. She knew every tree by heart and loved to watch them dance. There was nothing more graceful than a willow in the wind. The low, wispy branches nearly caressing the grass reminded her of the moss that hung from the trees in her Georgia backyard where she grew up. She rarely missed a Saturday afternoon on her bench, unless the winter weather was unbearable. She still hadn't gotten used to New England winters even though she had been there for over four years. Stealing away a few moments on Saturday afternoons replenished her. It gave her a chance to wander the willows, relax by the Swan Boats, and take pictures of nature, something she missed terribly. When she snapped those pictures, captured those natural moments, she was momentarily back home or transported to a simpler time. The photos were quiet compared to the city that surrounded the park.

On the verge of their first anniversary, she and Jonah prepared to go away to celebrate. Allie was anxious to get away from the city, the present. She wanted to get back to who she once was—free, full, uncomplicated, honest with the man she loved. As Allie ate and sipped tea while staring at the pond and swan boats drifting, she reminded herself of the old saying—the first year of marriage is the hardest. She and Jonah had weathered it nearly intact. Allie didn't let it escape her that they had made it through that first year because of her unwillingness to let Jonah in when she needed him most. Keeping him in the dark is what helped her maintain some semblance of light at the end of what felt like an ever-growing tunnel. She bore the burden of pain and emptiness as a means of keeping him full, light, and unscathed. Allie knew they wouldn't make it to their second anniversary by continuing to keep him safe from the truth. The truth can't be hidden or buried forever.

A squirrel ran to her feet, and a pigeon rested where the willow branches almost met the ground. Allie tore her crust in two and tossed it to both creatures. She smiled as they accepted her gift. Allie wiped her hands on her black jeans, sipped tea from her travel mug again, and then fiddled in her bag for her camera. She only had another hour before she needed to catch the T and head back to their apartment. There was packing to do. In the morning, Allie and Jonah would head back to the sight of their wedding a year earlier, back to Moose Pond Lodge in Great Pines, Maine.

As soon as the sun started to shine through their tiny bedroom window in the morning, Allie and Jonah scrambled to move their bags from the hallway and down three flights of stairs. Allie fought the temptation to toss her luggage down each flight.

"A third-floor walk-up was your idea, not mine," Jonah said as he slid one of her bags off her shoulder and onto his. "Give me that one, too. You worry about not falling down those stairs."

"I'm fine. I've got it, honey. And these stairs keep us both in shape, you know." Allie said with a laugh.

"Well, that's fine for now. But, if we have a kid soon, there's no way in hell we can stay here." Jonah unloaded the bags strapped to his shoulders and lowered the large suitcase. "Jesus, Al, what do you have in here? It's just two weeks." Allie made it to the bottom and lowered the bag she carried.

"You know it gets chilly there at night, so I have extra stuff. Like sweaters, jeans, I don't know. Oh, and there's a chance of rain this time. So, I have extra for that, too." Allie said. She fished for the car key in her pocket. Jonah smacked her on the ass.

"You certainly won't need to wear much at night." He smiled ear to ear. Allie laughed back.

"Just because it's our anniversary doesn't mean you're getting lucky, you know?" She pulled out the key from her faded black jeans. "There, finally. Let's get loaded up and out of Boston. Traffic is going to be a nightmare if we don't get on 95 soon."

The car meandered through the windy side streets, cobblestone one-way roads, and through countless stop signs and signals. Jonah unleashed his usual insults every other block as cars pulled out in front of him, stopped without warning, and honked relentlessly.

"Calm down, Jonah. You'll give yourself a heart attack if you keep it up all the way to the highway." Jonah blared the horn.

"We need to move out of the city, buy a house, get a yard, and get the hell off these city streets," Jonah said with a huff.

"I know. We will soon." Allie said. She grabbed onto the armrest as Jonah veered around another car. Both he and the other driver simultaneously blared their horns.

"Well, as soon as you get pregnant, we are definitely moving to the suburbs." Jonah squeezed her knee. She patted the top of his hand. Allie swallowed a lump in her throat. She wanted out of the city just as much as Jonah, even though she grew to love the home they created in that third-floor walk-up. It was cozy, not too cramped. It had a view of the harbor if you leaned far enough to the right, and it was easy to catch the T anywhere they wanted to go to Boston. She understood his urge to live in the suburbs. It was almost an ingrained next step for people their age once kids came along. But as much as she wanted a more peaceful existence, the suburbs weren't calling her like they did Jonah. She wanted more seclusion. She knew Jonah didn't. It made her cringe anytime he broached the subject anymore. *How can a couple make it fifty years if they can't decide where they want to live past year two?* Allie thought every time he mentioned the suburbs.

"Hey, maybe this weekend will be the one, you know?" Jonah squeezed again.

"Maybe it will," Allie said as she looked out the window.

"Don't be discouraged, Al. It'll happen for us soon. I just know it. Look at Darla and Jimmy. Jeez, my sister tried for what? Two years? Then boom, twins." Jonah laughed. "I still can't believe she has twins. I hope they act just like she did growing up. Best revenge ever." He squeezed again. "Hey? You hear me? Where are you, Allie?"

She turned his way and smiled. "I heard you. You're right. It'll happen sometime." Allie patted his hand again. She let the smile recede as she turned to the window again. "So, what time you think we'll get there? Wanna stop for lunch once we get across the border or what?"

"Sounds good to me. I'm craving a lobster roll." Jonah widened his eyes and grinned. He craned his neck as he merged onto the highway. The car roared as he hit the gas. Allie glanced over at him. She loved that look on his face every time he got on the highway. He loved to drive fast and let go once they left the city streets. She reached up and ran her hand through his sandy hair.

"I love you, Jonah Parker. You know that?"

Jonah reached up and drew her hand to his mouth. He kissed it gently. Then, bit her thumb. She squealed and pulled her hand back. "I love you, too. This weekend is gonna be great. You grabbed my tackle box, right? I can't wait to fish; I mean *really* fish."

"Yes, I got it. It's in the trunk."

With bellies full of seafood, they made their way through the last hour and half of the drive. It was all woods and quiet. There was an occasional car, but otherwise perfect stillness. Allie loved the idea that they weren't enclosed with thousands of others rushing about. There were no cement walls, horns honking at lights, flurries of cell phone conversations flooding her ears on every corner. Jonah opened the window slightly and stretched to smell the fresh air like a dog. Allie laughed. She rolled hers down slightly. There was no choking car exhaust or rumbling of bus brakes. There was silence, clean pine air, and green everywhere on either side of them. Allie watched as Jonah ingested so much air that his stomach rose. She envied his fullness, his obliviousness to the emptiness that plagued her the last few months.

Allie's heart quickened, and her mind let go of what she needed to forget as they made the turn into the resort driveway. She leaned forward and tapped Jonah's leg.

"It's just as beautiful as I remember. Oh, look! The gazebo, the porch, the rocking chairs. It's all so perfect. Oh, Jonah. I'm so glad we came back." Allie said.

Jonah turned the key. "Me too, Al. That was the best day ever. Best couple of days, actually. Come on. Let's say 'hi' and get our key."

They opened the car doors and stood on either side looking at the gazebo where they had exchanged vows a year earlier. Hanging plants swayed from the openings. Allie turned as she heard the screen door on the front porch slam shut.

"Molly!" she yelled as she rushed up the steps to hug Molly Watts. "You look incredible. My God, everything looks incredible." Allie drew Molly in close and squeezed her like a long-lost sister.

"Thanks. You look great, too. Of course. Hey Jonah! Welcome back, guys. Come on in and get signed in. I've got your cabin all ready." Molly slid her hand into Allie's as she reached for the door. Jonah followed them inside.

Allie's eyes climbed the stone wall to the moose antlers anchoring the fireplace. She let the smell of wood fill her lungs as she followed Molly to the front desk. Every detail of her wedding flashed through her mind, the candles lining the mantle, the pieces of cake, glasses of wine, and music flowing throughout the entire lodge. That day was magical, and Moose Pond Lodge was magical for Allie, also.

"You look so refreshed, like new, Molly," Allie said as Molly went behind the desk to flip through the guest book. She reached under for a key.

"Thanks, Allie. I feel it. I really do. I think it's plain old happiness. I've had an awesome year back here." Molly said through a broad smile. "Are you guys wanting to fish, hike, take pictures along the trail before dark or you just going to relax a little? How long was the drive, anyway?"

Allie drew her thick hair back and pulled her sunglasses off the top of her head. "It was what? About 5 hours today? Not too bad, I guess. I think we'll probably get settled then wander down to the water. What time is dinner?"

"6 o'clock sharp. There's a full menu in your cabin. Come on. I'll help you guys with your luggage if you want to walk down." Molly said as Jonah came up behind Allie. He kissed Allie's shoulder.

As the three of them made their way to the bridge and down the trail scattered with pine needles and cones with luggage in tow, Allie absorbed the sunshine, the sound of the birds swooping around, and the feel of the breeze in her hair. She told herself Jonah was right. This getaway was the perfect place and time for them to unwind, forget work, forget the city, and reconnect with nature and each other. Allie knew he had sensed a distance, too. While his attempts to bridge that gap were notably valiant and made her temporarily insane with passion for him, they were fleeting. After a date night or a night of unbridled ravaging of each other, she knew his mind and sometimes body were both back at work or focused on something else. He had a way of leaving her without leaving the room. It was as if the busyness of the city coursed through his veins. Her mind would wander to the secret that Jonah didn't even realize was the source of some of that distance.

Molly bounced along in front of her. "Tell me, Allie. How's the last year been? I've looked up some of your pictures online. Your work is amazing."

"Thank you so much. Life's been good in Boston, but I tell ya, it's so nice to be out of the city for a while. I'll never get used to the noise. It'll be awesome to wake up to birds, not sirens." Allie said as she dragged her large suitcase behind her. "How about your year? Are you happy you stayed? Where's Emerson, by the way?"

"She's in Nashville for the next few weeks with her dad. And, yeah. I'm certainly glad I stayed. It's been an adjustment being here with the knowledge that I'm in this for the long haul, but I think I made the right choice, thanks to you. I've worked super hard to get this place where it is now and reconnecting with the people I love in town helps, too. My old best friend, the others who work here, all feels like family again." Molly said.

Allie smiled at her. "How about the guy? The one with the truck?"

Allie looked up to see a man with floppy black hair emerge from the trail with an ax over his shoulder.

"Hey, Zack!" Molly yelled. "You remember meeting Allie and Jonah from last year? They're checking in for two weeks."

"Well, that answers my question," Allie said to Molly. A huge grin slid across Molly's face. Her cheeks turned red.

"Yeah, he's stuck around here with me."

Zack lowered the ax as he approached Molly, Allie, and Jonah. Jonah slid bags off his shoulder and extended his hand. "Hey, man. Yeah, I remember you guys. I was clearing a tree that fell from last week's storm. I'll catch up with you guys at dinner, okay?" Zack winked at Molly and hoisted the ax back up over his shoulder. Molly turned and watched him walk toward the bridge as Allie and Jonah picked up their bags again.

"So, does he live here? Is it serious?" Allie asked as they headed toward the clearing where a dozen cabins awaited guests.

"No, no, he doesn't live here. We keep it a little light. I guess that's the word. Casual." Molly said as the cabins came into view. The opening to the clearing was like a different world opening in the middle of a thick pine forest. "Here we are. You guys are in number four. Over there." She pointed with her head as she lowered a bag to retrieve the key. Allie walked up beside her as Jonah moved the bags to the tiny porch.

"Casual, huh? I don't know how you keep it casual with a man like that." Allie said as she nudged Molly's side.

"Best way to keep from getting hurt again," Molly said as she handed Allie her satchel. "Well, guys, I'm going back to the lodge. You have my number if you need anything at all. I'll see you at dinner, okay?" Molly said. Allie stepped in front of her and embraced her again.

"Thanks for everything, Molly. It's so good to be back here with you and back at Moose Pond Lodge." Allie said in a whisper. "You have no idea how much I need this right now." Molly hugged her back. "Happy anniversary, Allie. I'm so glad you're here, too." Molly whispered back to her. Allie let go and walked up the steps to the porch. She ran her hand across the top of the rocking chair and followed Jonah inside.

The light bounced off the white wood paneled walls, and the smell of flowers filled the room. There was a fresh bouquet of lavender mixed with a few roses on the nightstand. A blue, white, and yellow handmade quilt flanked the bed. It looked a lot like the one Molly had given them as a wedding present. The wood floors gleamed. They were freshly refinished.

"You can damn near see your reflection in the floors," Jonah said just as Allie was ready to say the same thing. Sometimes, she thought Jonah could read her mind. However, other times it was painfully obvious he couldn't. Allie walked up behind him and drew her long, thin arms around him. He held her hands and leaned his head back into her.

"It's perfect. All of it." He said. Jonah turned to face her and pulled her close for a kiss. He pulled her hips into his. She smiled as she kissed him harder. His kisses had a way of stopping time and slowing down her racing mind. She moaned as he kissed her harder. Jonah slowly walked her over to the bed. Before she could formulate another thought, they were on the bed still kissing as both slithered out of their clothes. "I can't wait until tonight," Jonah said as he bit her bottom lip. She giggled as she broke free and slid her shirt over her head. He grabbed her hips and pulled her down further on the bed. They made love quickly and fiercely as if it was forbidden and they could get caught at any moment. Instantly exhausted afterward, she rolled over next to him. Her long black hair stuck to his arm as sweat rolled from both their bodies. Within seconds, their muscles relaxed, and they melted into the bed. Allie reached for the quilt and pulled it to her breasts. Jonah bit her shoulder softly then kissed it. She was dizzy for a moment. She giggled.

"That was quick." She said. Jonah leaned over and kissed her slow while holding her face.

"I just had to have you now, Allie. I can never get enough of you." He said in her ear.

"I can't get enough of you either. Never will." She said. Allie drew in a deep breath as the fresh Maine air blew through the window. "Let's get dressed, go to the water." He kissed her neck and reached for his clothes. Allie loved each second he was kissing her. It was as if he was gently placing band-aids on every cut she had ever endured, covering and relieving each flicker of pain she felt, even if he didn't know it. Even though he usually left within seconds of making love, she lingered there in his essence. Allie knew he didn't mean to disappear into work, whatever task needed to be done. She relished in an afterglow enough for them both and then would go about her day. Maybe, she thought, during the quiet of these two weeks, he'd stay and relish in it too. Then, perhaps she'd have the chance to let him in fully. Maybe he'd find the time to let her.

Jonah stood and buttoned his pants. He reached back on the bed for his shirt. Allie sat up and pulled the quilt to her shoulders.

"Who knows. Maybe we just started our family. Wouldn't that be something? To know exactly when we created our first born?" Jonah asked. "You know, if we do conceive here, we gotta give it a name from here. Well, a middle name at least. What do you think?"

Allie inhaled and forced a smile. "I know, I know, I'm getting a little ahead of myself," Jonah said as he tapped her foot. He tucked in his shirt. "Come on. Get dressed so we can wander around. I'm going on the porch."

Allie reached under the quilt to find her clothes. She watched him walk out the door to the porch. Once the screen door banged shut, Allie rose and put on her bra and black tank top. She dragged her bath bag and jeans into the bathroom. Allie put her shampoo and make-up on the tiny counter. She reached in the bag and took out a disk of birth control pills. Allie ran her finger over the circle and days. She couldn't leave them out on the counter or in the bag to be seen if Jonah hunted for anything he might've forgotten. Allie opened the medicine cabinet. She saw an old first aid kit. It was a yellowed box. She opened it. Years of mustiness floated up to her nose. There were a few bandages that hadn't seen the outside of that box in a decade. There was a sling, and a few packets of aspirin surely expired. Allie slid the disc into the box behind the sling. She closed the cabinet door. She just wasn't ready to involve Jonah in what could be another failure, another unbearable disappointment, another loss of something they never actually had. She wasn't ready to involve Jonah in anything she didn't need to. If she could handle it herself, she simply did.

Allie joined Jonah outside. She adjusted her camera around her neck.

"Ready?" Jonah said as he slid his hand into hers. She nodded and squeezed his hand. They wandered down the trail to the pond.

"My God. That air, Jonah. It smells so clean. Wait." Allie said. She stopped and took a few shots of the tops of the trees. Jonah held his hand up to his forehead to block the sun.

"You want to frame some like you did from last year?" He asked. She nodded. "I really think you should do a calendar. I bet Molly would sell them in the lodge."

"Yeah, maybe she wants new pictures to hang up here, too?"

They made their way to the pond. There was complete silence. Jonah walked over to the canoe pulled up to the sandy beach. He lifted the paddle.

"Wanna take a ride around for a bit?"

"Yeah, why not. Just don't tip it and ruin my camera. This is my best one."

"Oh, come on. I'm the best canoe captain in New England." He propped his leg up on the edge and used the ore to steady himself. "Aye, ma lady. Join me on me vessel. Let's pillage Maine and make love on a pile of riches." Allie laughed as she walked towards him. She saluted.

"I'll pillage the earth with you, my dear captain. Does this make me your first mate?" She said as he stepped aside to push the canoe half into the water.

"Forever." He offered her his hand, and she stepped into the canoe. Jonah threw his shoes off and rolled up his pants. He pushed the canoe in further and jumped in with her. He grabbed the paddle and pressed down into the sand to steady it. Allie squealed with laughter as the canoe swayed side to side.

"I swear, if we tip over and I lose this camera, I'm gonna be eternally pissed at you!" He pulled the other paddle from under their seats and winked at her as he started to row them away from the beach.

"I got this, honey. Lean back, relax."

"I know you do. You always do. You always have everything under control. You're the steadiest man I've ever known." She said as she leaned back. Allie pulled down her sunglasses as she scanned the sky. A bird swooped overhead. She saw gnats swirl in a cloud not far above her head. The sound of the water being pierced rhythmically, and the slight rock of the boat filled her with peace. Everything in her world was a constant, at least for the moment. Each subtle splash was timed perfectly as Jonah rowed. Just like everything else about him, his rowing was steady, methodical, and dependable. Allie knew he'd always keep her afloat, even if he didn't realize how close she was to going under. He'd always keep their boat steady and protect her from anything that might upend all they had. Allie wondered if she was able to do the same for him, or if her truth would capsize all they had built, leaving them both floundering in the waters below.

As Jonah rowed and rattled off his plans for each day, Allie found herself getting lost in his voice. His surety was something she absolutely loved about him, but at the same time, that steadiness and surety made telling him anything that would rock the boat even more difficult. Her life had been full of 'rock the boat moments' before he walked in and laid a solid course at her feet. He had his life outlined in steps, a measurable procession of accomplishments and goals. There were no exit signs, no backroads to make him lose his way, no tidal waves, or storms to veer them off course. Allie knew if she had met him a year or even a day earlier than she had, she would've been bored to tears by these traits. She wouldn't have given him a second thought. But, Jonah and all that he was walked up to her at the right moment.

Allie sat up all the way and pulled her sunglasses back to the top of her head when she heard him stop talking. He tilted his head to the side.

"You didn't hear a word I said, did you?" Jonah said as he rowed within feet of the beach. Pine needles clung to the oars.

"What? Maybe. I don't know. But, I was thinking about you if that gets me a pass for zoning off?" Allie said. Jonah rolled up his pants and stepped out of the canoe.

"Hang on. I'll pull it in closer." Jonah said. "And see, I didn't get your camera wet." He reached out his hand to help her out.

"I knew you wouldn't, Mr. Parker."

"Let's get ready for dinner, Mrs. Parker."

Allie lingered behind taking more shots as they wandered back to their cabin. She took a few of Jonah in front of her, leading the way like he always did.

Once they changed and made their way to the main lodge, memories of their wedding day flooded Allie's mind. She could almost feel the silk of her dress tickle under her arm. It was a perfect moment in her life, and she knew Jonah did everything possible to make sure every moment since was perfect as well.

As they walked in, her eyes went straight to the moose antlers high on the stone mantle.

"Hey, you guys made it. Come in. Sit." Molly called out from the other side of the fireplace. She hugged them both as they made their way into the dining room.

"There's no band tonight but will be tomorrow night when I've got a few more people arriving for the week," Molly said. "I'll be right back." She darted off to the kitchen. As the double doors swayed, Allie and Jonah sat across from each other at the wooden table closest to the kitchen. Allie unfolded her napkin and ran her fingers across the knots in the table. Jonah reached down and took her hand. He kissed it just as Molly re-emerged with a tray of water, tea, and glasses. She poured both for them and sat beside Allie.

"So, tell me everything about the last year and Boston. I rarely, if ever, make it into Portland to get the rush of city life again. I miss it, but this place has kept me so busy."

"Boston is Boston. I'm still at The Herald taking pictures of crime scenes, council meetings, and everything else I don't want to capture through a lens." Allie said with a laugh.

"Well, I'm sure you'll enjoy taking nature pictures around here the next two weeks."

"Oh, speaking of which, Molly, would you be interested in updating the framed pictures you have hanging up around here? I mean, Jonah has this idea that maybe I do a calendar of my pictures and your resort would be a great location."

"Oh, my goodness, ask no more. Take all the pictures you want. I'd love to buy a few to hang in the main lodge and cabins. I love the ones that are there, but I've been trying to update as much as I can. Emerson and I have spent the last year making this place more *our* home rather than just the place that was *my* childhood home." Molly said.

"I can tell you redid the floors. They look great." Jonah said as he poured more iced tea.

"Well, that was mostly Zack," Molly said.

"Mostly? Really Mol?" Zack yelled out as he came through the double doors with a tray of food.

"What? I helped some." Molly said with a huge smile. She stood and kissed Zack's cheek as he put down the tray. Zack and Jonah shook hands again as Zack took a seat.

"So, Jonah, your work still growing in Boston?" Molly asked as they passed a large bowl of salad.

"Yes, too much actually. I used to have the choice to work from home here and there, but now I need to be there every day, some weekends too. And, we've opened up a larger office in Lexington, right along the 95 corridor." Jonah said as he reached for corn on the cob dripping with butter.

"Basically, he is the only guy commuting *from* the city *to* the suburbs," Allie said with a laugh.

"Yeah, it's not ideal at the moment. But, things will change when we have a family. I think we'll either move out there and get the typical yard, picket fence whole deal, or I'll get something else in the city, and we'll stay put."

"I don't think we'll stay put either way. I need trees. It's bad enough I have to take the T across town to go sit under the willows every weekend just to remember what grass feels like." Allie quipped as she poured more tea.

"Oh, come on. It's not that bad. There's plenty of green spaces in Boston besides the Public Garden and Common. You're being a little dramatic."

"Dramatic? I just want something quieter, softer under us, you know?" Allie said.

"Yeah, I do too. We'll figure that out when we have to, like when a kid is on the way." Jonah said with a wink. Smiles came across everyone's faces except for Allie.

"Well, I don't see why we have to wait until we have a kid to move somewhere without concrete in every direction." She looked down. "I mean, there's no guarantee we'll have a kid anytime soon. We can afford to move now. Why wait for something that might never happen?" Jonah put down his fork and squinted.

"Might not ever happen? We just started trying, Allie. Don't sound so pessimistic."

Zack cleared his throat. Allie looked up at him, letting him know she was thankful for the interruption. A quiet fell over the table.

"So, Zack. You work here or just, how should say it? Play here?" All four laughed. Molly blushed.

"Well, I still have a landscaping business. I do some work for a few companies in the county, but I'm technically the property manager here, for the summer at least. Unless, of course, I quit over the sexual harassment." He raised his eyebrows at Molly.

"Hey, wait now. That goes both ways, Zack." Molly said before taking another bite. "Yes, he's my property manager. I quickly learned by the end of the season last year that I needed more help to run this place. At least, more hands-on help in the summer. In the winter, I've got it myself, except for the plowing by this guy of course." Molly said. "Once I got my feet on the ground after your wedding and decided I definitely wasn't selling, I put everything into this place, and it started to show. I was booked solid until the end of October. I made enough to invest in upgrades and market this place for winter events, too. Zack was a huge help with that. We had a few winter weddings and even added gas heat to the cabins instead of relying on space heaters here and there."

She put more salad on her plate. "I'm booked solid for this summer, too. Another couple and a few families arrive tomorrow. If it weren't for Zack, I'd totally be in over my head."

"So, you two are together?" Allie asked. Zack shot Molly a look.

"Yep. She likes to say we're keeping it casual. But, I'm not. There's nothing casual about this for me." Zack reached across the table and tapped Molly's hand.

"A little sure of yourself, aren't you?" Molly said. "I told you, I'm just in it for the sex." Zack laughed as Molly winked at him.

"Lucky man," Jonah said.

"Same reason I married this guy," Allie said as she pointed her fork at Jonah. "Just wanted that body for myself," Jonah smirked.

"I knew it." He said.

"Well, she may be in it for the sex, but I'm in for the long haul," Zack said.

"Zack. Quit." Molly said. Jonah cleared his throat. Silence draped the four of them for a few moments.

"So, Allie, about those pictures," Molly said. "How much would it cost me to purchase a few, say 12 by 15 photos for framing? Or whatever you think is a good size for the walls."

"Well, definitely a discount for you," Allie said. "I'll email you a link where you can see some prices."

The two couples finished dinner. As Zack and Molly cleared the table, Molly told them to wander to the lounge for drinks if they wanted. When they joined them, Molly stepped behind the bar and tied on an apron. The bartender, Carl, was washing glasses. Allie and Jonah sat on bar stools and fiddled with the newspaper from Great Pines. The smell of the wood bar rekindled memories of sitting there last summer.

"Way smaller than the Herald, huh?" Molly said.

"Yeah, but the pictures are good. People don't realize there's just as much talent on the pages of a small town paper as there is in a big city newsroom. It's the same business regardless of the size of the audience." Allie said. "I'd love to work at a small-town paper. I love the Herald, but my pictures get lost in the shuffle. I get lost in the shuffle." Jonah tapped her hand.

"What do you want to drink, guys?" Molly asked.

As the drinks flowed, Allie's laugh got louder, and Jonah's cheeks got redder. Zack helped Molly clean up the bar once Carl left for the night. A few other couples sat at tables across from the bar.

"Say, Molly. Why don't you sit down, have a drink?" Allie said.

"Nah. I have a glass of wine here and there, but other than that, I don't drink anymore," Molly said. She wiped the bar around Allie's beer.

"But, I do," Zack said as he opened a beer and walked to the other side of the bar. "It helps me deal with my boss." Molly whipped her dish towel at his arm.

"What do you two have planned for tomorrow?" Molly asked.

"I want to do some fishing, a hike maybe. Read on the porch. As long as I don't have to drive to do it." Jonah said. Allie smiled at him.

"I want to sleep in, read on the porch, too. And take some pictures of course." Allie said.

"Well, once I get tomorrow's guests settled, I can join you, Allie, if you want? I'd love to wander around while you take pictures. Catch up more?" Molly said.

"I'd love that. It's a date."

"Our first anniversary and you're ditching me and making dates with a beautiful woman," Jonah said as he took the last swig of his beer.

"She's irresistible. Plus, I have no desire to fish, and you know it." Allie took the last sip of her beer. "Can we get a few bottles to go? You ready to relax in our cabin?" She said to Jonah.

Molly handed them both two beers and an opener to take. "Be careful on the trail. It's pretty dark out there."

Allie winked at Molly and gathered her long black hair to one side.

"Don't you worry about me. I grew up in the woods of Georgia running alongside copperheads and rattlesnakes. This city boy is the one who can't make it in the woods at night." She took her two bottles in one hand and slid her free arm under Jonah's as they left the lounge.

As they made their way to their cabin, Allie kept looking up at the stars.

"God, I miss seeing so many stars. It's so clear here. Everything is clearer here."

"Well, you know, you can't see them much in the suburbs either. Just as many street lights there, too."

"Yeah, I know. Sadly. We don't have to live in a city or suburb forever." She said. She swayed as she walked.

"Watch where you're going, love. You're gonna walk right off that bridge and land in the creek." Jonah said as he reached for her hand. "I thought you wanted to move to the suburbs soon, too. We'll have a yard, some grass, maybe even plant a willow tree like the ones you love in the park."

"That does sound lovely, definitely lovelier than being surrounded by concrete and feeling like I can't breathe with all those buildings closing in on me. But, why is it only a choice of Boston or the Boston suburbs? Why haven't we thought of leaving urban areas altogether? You know, those aren't the only two choices. I grew up in the country, and I turned out fine."

"Leave my job in the city and do what? Fish all day? No one is gonna pay me to fish in the country while you stare up at the stars. Plus, you love your job, too, well for the most part." He squeezed her hand. "Al, we've got decades ahead of us. I don't think we need to decide this tonight, do we?"

"No, we don't. I just miss it. Living near woods, grass, and all. I feel like I'm suffocating in Boston. I really do, Jonah."

"I know you do. But aren't you being a little dramatic? Anyways, it's not like I dragged you from some idyllic wide-open farm to the depths of the city filled with crimes, gangs, and all. You chose to live there before you even met me. You were certainly happy being a single in the city kind of girl. Why's that all changing now?"

"I don't know. I guess I just feel trapped there. And yeah, I loved it once. I do love it now for the most part. That doesn't mean I don't miss where I grew up. This place reminds me of home, that's all. I can breathe here. Hey,

I'm just tipsy and sentimental right now." He stopped and drew her in front of him.

"I love when you're sentimental. And, most of the time, I love when you're tipsy. We'll figure it all out. I promise. But for right now, we have the stars, the quiet, the woods, and everything else you love right here." Jonah said.

He kissed her. Usually one to close her eyes during his kisses, Allie peered one eye open and spotted the stars in the distance. Kissing Jonah under a star-filled sky, in the woods, in the silence, was perfection. It was the kind of perfection she knew wouldn't last. It seemed lately, every moment of bliss or perfection was immediately followed by flashes of how it could all fall apart when she told him about the miscarriage. Or, worse yet, it could all fall apart if she couldn't or didn't get pregnant again. The worst part of those fears was the idea that he'd look at her differently from that moment forward. She didn't want him to look at her as she now saw herself, empty and a failure at the one thing they both needed her to be.

Despite those fleeting fears, Allie dove into any of those perfect moments head first. She knew how to let those fears go or at least, push them aside until after the perfect moment passed or he got up from the bed after they made love. Allie was an expert at compartmentalizing her life. Just as she looked through a lens of her camera and focused on the frame, the shot, she did so in life. She could zoom in on what she wanted to feel, to let in, then zoom back out for the whole picture when she wanted. Allie could cut out what she didn't want to see or capture in any shot of her life. By keeping Jonah in the dark, keeping the truth out of the frame, she was also controlling what was in Jonah's frame, what he saw of her.

Allie knew that was wrong, but she knew no other way to keep his view of her, of their life, the way it was in his mind. The truth would make the entire shot blurry, muddled, and dark. She didn't want that for herself, much less for him.

After they made their way to the cabin porch, they sat together in silence finishing the beers. Each rocked back and forth and stared at the stars. She listened to him breath slower. It was the most relaxed he'd been in months. She listened as their entire world slowed a bit. He reached for her hand and led her inside. They made love in the cabin much slower than they had in the afternoon. Jonah caressed every inch of Allie's long, tanned body. They didn't speak a word. She drank him in, his scent, his breath. They were intertwined and still afterward. Allie let her body melt into his and the bed. She felt paralyzed by the peace and fullness, a rarity anymore. She would've gladly remained in that bed in the middle of the Maine woods with him forever. For the first time in a long time, her world was suspended on its axis. She floated above everything that had consumed her the last few months. Then, those little fears started to creep back in just as she could see Jonah slip into a deep sleep with his arm still on her hip.

As she lingered on the edge of sleep, she remembered. Allie slid from beneath Jonah and went into the bathroom. She gently closed and locked the door behind her. Allie winced as the medicine cabinet door creaked. She opened the old first aid kit and took out her pack of birth control pills. Allie popped one from the foil and quickly swallowed it. She closed the cabinet door and stared at herself in the mirror. She ran her hands through her tangled, long black hair. She squeezed her eyes tight enough to prevent a tear from falling. Allie's palms started to sweat. She never intended to lie to Jonah. She never planned to keep him in the dark, to cut him from the frame of what were her hardest moments. She wanted to give him a child more than anything. He deserved to be a dad, and she wanted that for him as much as she wanted it for herself. But, Allie couldn't try, not yet, not now, not until she could work up the nerve to tell him about April and zoom out enough to let in the truth. She not only lost their child, but she also chose to keep it to herself and cut him from the shot entirely. She wasn't sure what the truth would do to him, to them, once the full picture developed.

Chapter Two

Simone

Simone studied herself in the mirror of the passenger seat. She dabbed under her eyes with a tissue and ran a brush through her fine, fiery hair. Simone's sky-blue eyes grew wide as she spotted a few wispy strands protruding from her crown.

"Oh my God, Ethan."

"What? What's wrong?" her husband said as he glanced back and forth between Simone and the road.

"It's a grey hair. A god-damned grey hair sticking straight up like it's trying to get the world's attention. It's practically screaming 'look at me!'" Ethan laughed as Simone repeatedly tried to pat the strand down. "Jesus, there's another one." She said. Simone turned and leaned her head down towards Ethan. He laughed at her.

"It's fine. You are 42, you know. You can always dye it."

"I just had my color refreshed two weeks ago!" she said as she sat back up. Ethan laughed at her again.

She smirked back at him as she rummaged through her purse for lip gloss. They were about 10 minutes away from Moose Pond Lodge. Simone was nervous about the northern Maine retreat Ethan had raved about the last month. She hadn't set foot in any sort of wilderness since she was a kid unless you counted strolling the gardens of historic homes in her hometown of Greenwich, Connecticut. Even those obligatory historical society excursions resulted in more dirt on her shoes than she was comfortable with.

Her family beach house was as outdoorsy as she willingly dared to get on a regular basis. Simone loved the feel of sand under feet, in-between her toes, and even stuck to her legs. The sea was wild, enticing, almost like a forbidden fruit but in the wide open. Woods were a different story. There was too much unknown, too much hidden for her liking. It took Ethan months to convince her that a getaway in northern Maine would do them some good. His career as a financial advisor in Manhattan meant he was gone from sun up to sun down. Her charity work and family obligations took up her weekends. They were living parallel lives, traveling the same direction on different roads, only seeing each other across the median when there was a break in the scenery.

Once he convinced her to give Moose Pond Lodge a chance, she spent an entire month researching supplies. She ordered every possible piece of equipment from L.L. Bean---shoes, boots, socks, camping flashlights, a battery-powered radio, flannel shirts, a classic barn coat, even a compass. Ethan had to explain they wouldn't really be camping, but staying in a cabin, with electricity, running water, a fireplace, and a claw foot tub. She loaded her gear into a new, oversized duffle bag just in case. While she felt slightly foolish when she read the website and realized they weren't going to be roughing it in any way, Simone still wanted to be prepared. There wasn't a moment in Simone's adult life where she didn't dedicate herself to being unapologetically prepared. Well, there were a few moments tucked away in the corners of her mind.

She ran lip gloss across her pale pink lips, noticing a few more wrinkles and freckles than she had before. She had already gone the Botox route like nearly all her friends, but maybe she'd inquire about some injections when they returned. While a grey hair or two might've been a laughing matter, Simone was not going to succumb to the aging process on her face. It was all she had for so many years. It was what set her apart, made her special, and in her mind, made her worthy of the riches that had been bestowed on her for as long as Simone could remember. She had been a model from the time she could stand on a stage until after she married Ethan Beckwith. Her marriage to him ushered out her modeling career and ushered in her career as a socialite, charity diva, and arm candy of one of the wealthiest men in Greenwich. She had been much more than that for one exotic and dangerous year of her life. But, being with Ethan for the last 15 years and playing the role mapped out by him and her family was what she was good at, even though she momentarily risked losing it all in April.

They pulled into the driveway of Moose Pond Lodge, and Simone's eyes once again grew wide. She gasped.

"Oh, come on, Simone. It's not that remote or rustic."

"No, no, it's not that," she said as she craned her head to see more of the main lodge from the windshield. "It's gorgeous. I didn't expect it to be so, so, lovely looking." She smiled and tapped his knee. Her heart quickened, a sensation she hadn't felt in a while. Ethan walked around and opened her door, as he always did. She took his strong hand. She glanced at his fingers as they wrapped around her own. Simone always thought Ethan had the strong hands of a man who could tolerate rough manual labor even though he was the very type who would never know what that was. She slid out of the car. Simone suddenly didn't mind that she was standing on gravel. The sun hit her face. She briefly thought about her freckles and pulled down her sunglasses.

"Let's check in and get settled in our cabin," Ethan said. He led her up the steps to the two large wooden doors. As Ethan reached for the wrought iron handles, the door delicately creaked. A short, bouncy blonde appeared.

"Hey there. Welcome to Moose Pond Lodge. I'm Molly. You guys must be the Beckwiths?" She said as she turned and walked toward a tall stand near the back wall. Simone's eyes scanned the stone fireplace and widened as she stopped at the moose antlers. They engulfed all the air and space above her. Simone slid her sunglasses to the top of her head and let her purse slide down her arm.

"That's the most massive set of antlers I've ever seen. My grandfather went on safari long before I was born and has similar antlers in his study from various animals, but they aren't nearly as expansive as those." Simone said.

"Yes, that's one of the biggest sets in Maine. Well, that's what I was told as a kid, at least. My father bagged it when I was a baby, I think. Let's get you checked in, and I'll show you your cabin." Molly said as she slid behind the stand and picked up a pen with one hand and pamphlets with the other. "Now, there's plenty to do and see around here, in town, around the resort. I can give you directions, too. Here's a menu for the week and a list of a handful of restaurants in Great Pines. We have drinks in the lounge every night, too. The specials are on there, too." Molly handed the stack to Ethan as he nodded and fiddled through his wallet for his credit card. "I gotta warn you though. They are calling for a pretty big storm later in the week, so keep that in mind when deciding what you want to do when."

"Oh, okay," Ethan said. He handed the stack to Simone. She slid them into her oversized leather tote bag.

"We can drive down the trail, over a bridge, to your cabin if you're ready?" Molly said. She scribbled in the book, making a check mark next to the name Beckwith.

"Can we walk? I mean, I'd rather walk there than drive." Simone said. Ethan snapped his head around at her.

"Walk? It's a dirt trail, Simone. We have a lot of luggage, too."

"I'd like to walk. I'm not allergic to dirt, you know." She said as she smiled at Molly.

"Sure, we can walk. It isn't that far. I have utility wagons I use to haul stuff to the cabins. We can load one up if you don't mind pulling it, Mr. Beckwith?" Molly said.

"Mr. Beckwith is my dad. Please call me Ethan. Yep, I'll pull it."

The lanky couple cascaded down the steps as Molly brought a cart around. Simone took her duffle bag out of the trunk.

"I'll get that," Ethan said. Simone slung it over her shoulder.

"I've got it." She stepped away from the car as Ethan placed bags in the cart.

"What's with the independent act?" He said. Simone felt a slight piercing pain in her gut. "Who are you trying to impress?"

Simone let the duffle bag slide down her arm. She lowered it into the wagon. She glanced up at Ethan, then back down to the ground as she pulled her sunglasses back over her eyes. "No one, Ethan. No one." Ethan tugged the wagon. Simone followed behind. His freshly pressed khakis were as blinding as the sun.

Molly told them the history of the lodge, the pond, and where each trail led to as she unfolded a pamphlet with a small map in the bottom corner. Simone smiled and nodded. She didn't hear a word Molly said but was hypnotized by her enthusiasm and ease as she strode across the bridge and the trail. Simone couldn't help but think how out of her element she must seem to someone like Molly. Simone glanced down at her boots. Surely Molly must notice they are brand-spanking-new. Everything she had on was new, stiff, too clean for that trail and real life. Simone glanced Molly up and down. To Simone, she looked comfortable, natural. Ethan could pull off the rugged look and attitude, even in new clothes. He did go fishing in Wisconsin and white water rafting in New Hampshire a few times a year. Suddenly, Simone's guided tours of perennial herb and flower gardens seemed frivolous.

As she trailed behind Molly and Ethan, Simone wondered if everything about her seemed frivolous in Molly's eyes, in everyone's eyes. She glanced up and could almost hear her parents' voices outlining who she was, what she could be, and her role in their family and the world. There was no choice, no discussion of dreams, desires, or aspirations. There simply was her lot in life, the expectations they had for her. Any straying from that version of herself was shut down immediately and with brute force. The one time in her life where she tasted freedom from them, their expectations, and everything she knew was her junior year of college. It wasn't talked about. It was only referred to in whispers. It was what they called her 'breakdown.' Little did her parents or Ethan know another 'breakdown' was bubbling up inside of Simone. She could taste it but kept swallowing it back down since April. However, she knew it was going to come out sooner or later. And, it would be a truth none of them could stomach. Rich girls from Greenwich don't do what she did, and they certainly don't do it twice.

The trail opened to the clearing with cabins scattered in a semi-circle. Simone gasped again. Molly reached over and touched her arm.

"It's quite beautiful, isn't it? Much different than the city." Molly whispered.

"Exactly. Much different than everything in my life." Simone spun in a circle. She felt dizzy for a moment as she tried to take in the entire view all around her. The cabins, clearing, wildflowers, and the towering trees behind them engulfed her. There was one lone willow in the clearing in front of two of the cabins. She inhaled. Simone didn't want to exhale any of it. She wanted to keep it in forever. Even the sun felt different.

"Well, that's it. Number three is yours." Molly said. Simone shook her head and tried to steady herself.

"Number three sounds wonderful." She said. Ethan glanced at her. He tilted his head as if to study a creature he'd never seen before. Simone looked away.

"Wow. This is even better than online." Ethan said as he placed luggage on the bed. Molly grabbed one of Simone's bags and put it on the chair next to the fireplace.

"Thank you," Simone said. She took a fistful of bills from her tote bag. She took Molly's hand. Molly pulled back.

"Oh, no, no. That's not necessary. I own the place. You can surely tip the girls who clean if you'd like. But, not me." She said with a chuckle.

"Sorry. I'm a little out of my element here." Simone said as she slid the money back in her bag.

"A little?" Ethan shot back at her as he opened his luggage. Simone felt the all-too-familiar pierce of his words. His idea of a joke was her idea of humiliation. While he might not have meant it to be, he could slip into being 'that guy' in an instant, and always when Simone needed him not to be. Cocktail parties, company trips, holiday get-togethers with both their families, anytime really, except when they were alone.

After Molly left them alone in the cabin, Ethan settled into a rocking chair on the porch. Simone aligned her clothes in the closet and methodically stacked her toiletries before joining him. She swayed back and forth as her eyes scanned the sky. Both with long legs, they swayed nearly in unison.

"I'm glad you talked me into coming here. Believe it or not, I really think it's lovely. Lovelier than I imagined." She said into the air above her.

"I told you you'd like it. That tub is awesome. Very retro. Maybe we should buy a place like this? A cabin or something in the woods away from the city."

"We've got the beach house. That's a perfect escape."

"Yeah for you, maybe. Not for me. I'm lucky if I get to stay there more than a weekend in the summer."

"Well, that's not my fault. And, it's not like you'd be around more if we got some cabin in the woods. You don't even have to work so much. Jesus, your dad owns the company. You can certainly take more vacation days."

"It's because my dad owns it that I've got to work more. You know that." Ethan said. He stopped rocking. "Plus, you never seem to mind going there alone. In fact, you seem to relish in it lately." She slowed her rocking. He was right. She did relish in her time alone at her family's beach house in the Hamptons. She had since she was a kid. Both her parents' families, the Sterns and Forresters, had acquired tons of land along Sag Harbor and Montauk, back during a time when the peninsula didn't mean much to anyone outside of the upper echelon of Manhattan. Their investment paid off after of four generations. At one point, the two families joined together through her parents' marriage owned more land than any other family in the Hamptons. The Sterns-Forrester beach house was anything but quaint.

"Let's hike before dinner, my dear," Ethan said as he pushed himself up from the white, creaky chair. "Enough talk about work and a beach house hundreds of miles away. Let's enjoy being here while we're here." Again, he presented his hand for her taking. And again, per usual, she took it and pulled herself up to his level.

As they left the clearing and entered the first trail, Simone glanced at her boots. She knew they would get dirty and, for the first time in two decades, she was excited to expose herself to a little grit. She clutched the map of the trails in her hand and reached for Ethan with the other. The trail ascended as the trees grew thicker. Simone couldn't remember a time in her life when she was so immersed in green. She glanced around. There was no peak of a building. There were no cars in the distance. There wasn't even the sound of other people picnicking or splashing in a fountain like in Central Park and the city parks of Greenwich. There was periodic rustling of the unknown, treetops clustered and melted into other treetops, and most of all, there was silence. Simone could hear herself and Ethan breathe. She could hear her footsteps and the sound of the earth being displaced below her brand-spanking-new boots. She could feel the slight sink as the dirt and needles enveloped her long stride. Simone smiled. She had a fleeting thought that the trail, the woods, the earth was accepting her. There weren't too many times in life when she felt any semblance of acceptance.

Simone opened the map as they came to a fork. Ethan let go of her hand and placed his hands on his hips.

"Which way, my love?"

"Hang on. Let me check where we are." Simone uttered with the map directly in front of her face. Ethan grabbed it. He loosely folded it under his arm.

"Seriously, Simone. We aren't even a quarter mile from the cabin. There's no wrong choice. Either path will get us to the pond and back to our cabin." He said. She knew he was right. She nodded her head to the left. It looked more wooded. She was suddenly feeling the urge to be more immersed.

Simone was so busy scanning the treetops, she barely noticed the pond came into view until Ethan stopped dead in his tracks.

"Well, look at that. That's Maine. Every postcard, calendar, picture I've ever seen. Maine, plain and simple. God, it's gorgeous, huh?"

Simone slid next to him. She drew in another deep breath and let her eyes absorb the view. A bird swooped past and glided over the pond. The water sparkled and swayed with the slight breeze. She felt dizzy again.

"Gorgeous it is." She said. "How is it that I'm 42 and just now seeing this view? This place?" Ethan smirked.

"Come with me fishing in Wisconsin sometime, sweetie, and you'll see some more of this."

Nothing about being on a river in Wisconsin ever seemed appealing to Simone. Then again, until that afternoon, nothing about Maine did either. She stood up a little taller, losing her trademark slouch. Simone relaxed her hands by her side. She noticed for the first time in a long time she wasn't fidgeting. Her hands weren't balled up, twisted in a knot, or sore from squeezing. Her hands were at ease. She was at ease.

Once Ethan glanced at his watch, Simone knew it was time to make their way to the cabin to prepare for dinner. Her mind raced with what to wear and how to wear it. Ethan reached back for her hand as the approached the clearing and cabin, her home for the next weeks.

"Don't fret. It's not like a formal dinner affair." Ethan said as he opened the cabin. She squinted at Ethan and the absurdity of his comment. The fact that it wasn't formal was exactly why she'd fret. He laughed. She suddenly realized he was trying to joke with her. After more than ten years of marriage, Simone still wasn't instantly sure when Ethan was kidding or not until he gave her a subtle clue.

Simone fingered through the outfits she had hanging in the small closet. She held up a pair of black pants and a crisp, white linen shirt. She changed. Simone stood in front of the bathroom and fidgeted as she stared at herself. Her mind raced with which necklace to wear and which pair of flats would pair best. She gasped when she realized they had walked to the cabin rather than drove. This meant her flats would surely get dusty. "Well, that rules out the glittery Choo's. Dammit." She murmured to herself. "Screw it. I'll have them cleaned when I get home." She shrugged her shoulders and ran a brush through her red hair again. She remembered standing in front of a mirror in her mother's bedroom, getting her hair brushed, braided, and fly-aways smoothed every morning. It was a ritual, as was most of her childhood, her life. She ran sparkly lip gloss over her lips and freshened her mascara. Simone draped her turquoise and silver necklace over her crisp linen. "Ah, yes. This is a bit rustic. It'll work." She spritzed herself with jasmine. After one more head to toe glance, Simone emerged from the bathroom. Ethan, in jeans and a polo, reached for her hand and led her to the main lodge.

As they wound around the floor to ceiling stone fireplace, the smell of fried chicken engulfed her. She felt a twinge in the pit of her stomach thinking this might mean eating with her fingers, grease on her arm, a stain on her crisp linen shirt.

"There you guys are!" Molly's chipper voice called out as she broke through the double doors. "Have a seat at the long table with Allie and Jonah." Molly nodded to the table as she balanced a tray. She quickly shuffled glasses of iced tea to a table of five—two parents and three small children, one of which was in a high chair. Molly glided across the dining room. She made it to the table before Ethan and Simone did.

"Allie, Jonah, this is Ethan and Simone, from Connecticut. The Beckwiths. Beckwiths, this is Allie and Jonah Parker. They were married here last summer and came back for their first anniversary." Molly said as she slid out chairs.

"Greenwich. We're from Greenwich." Simone said. Allie nodded as she wiped her hands. She stretched her long tan arm out to Simone to shake.

"Boston. We're from Boston." Allie said as she swallowed. Jonah stood and shook Ethan's hand.

"Quite a grip, man. You play football or something?" Jonah said as he looked up at Ethan.

"A little. In prep and a year at Brown." Ethan said.

"So, Simone. If I had to guess, I'd say you're a supermodel." Allie said as Simone took a seat. Simone laughed.

"No, not quite." She giggled. "I did a little modeling in my younger years. But supermodel? Not even close."

"A little? She modeled her whole life until we got married." Ethan said as he poured iced tea from a picture.

"Younger years, huh? You don't look a day over thirty." Allie said. She picked up another piece of chicken from the platter in the center of the table.

Simone shot Allie a smile and nod as a silent 'thank you' for the compliment. She glanced around the table, unsure of what to do first. There wasn't a soup spoon, salad fork, or appetizer plate. It was simplistic, too simplistic. She wrung her hands as her eyes darted at everyone's plate.

"If I were you, I'd take a little bit of the coleslaw first. Then, a breast you can cut into." Allie said in a faint voice from across the table as the men talked about Brown versus Boston College. Simone swallowed a lump in her throat and nodded again. Simone had only known Allie for mere minutes but was already sure she'd need and appreciate her guidance. Simone picked at her chicken and dabbed her mouth with her napkin in between bites as she listened to Allie's stories of growing up in Georgia. She let herself be drawn into Allie's world of the fast-paced newsroom, stories of downloading and resizing pictures for a cover ready to print in seconds, and the gruesome details of her photos for an expose' on homelessness in Boston in the winter. Simone clutched her necklace as she pictured a mother with four children living in a car by the back bay, wrapped in worn blankets, posing for a picture for the cover of the Herald.

"That must feel amazing. Having your pictures on the cover for the world to see. With your name and all?" Simone said.

"Yeah, it is, I guess. A cover picture isn't the norm for me, trust me. I'm usually page 20, city council meetings, a few crime scenes. I don't even get the body shots." Allie said with a laugh. "I get the smashed store window shots." She tilted her head and shrugged her shoulders. "But, it's good money. I prefer nature photography. I'm thinking of doing my own calendar and Molly here has asked me to do some pictures for the resort."

"Ah, that sounds lovely and fun. I guess there aren't too many nature shots to be had in downtown Boston, right?"

"Well, actually I go to the public garden on the weekends and take pictures of the willows, the swans, the flowers. It's my favorite place."

"She'd live there if she could," Jonah said as he nudged Allie's side. "Just like here. She's a country girl through and through." He kissed her cheek.

"True story." She said back to him.

"I admire that. It must've been fun growing up like that. A calendar sounds amazing. I'd love to see your work sometime. I decorate and stage homes for my parents' real estate business in the Hamptons and Greenwich. I'm always looking for new pieces to add."

"Wow, really? I'd love to show you some. Maybe tomorrow? That sounds like a fun job, too. Exciting, different." Allie said.

"No, not really. I mean, yes, it's fun to stage and decorate for potential clients, but it's not necessarily an art form."

"Everything can be an art form if you do it with some passion and purpose," Allie said. Simone smiled at her. As they ate and as she listened to Allie tell more stories of her work, Simone couldn't help but notice how toned and tan she was. Allie looked like the kind of girl who never sat inside on a sunny day. She never had to douse herself in sunblock to avoid freckling. She was naturally exotic—something never said about Simone. Allie was the kind of woman who didn't need to spritz herself with jasmine to feel alluring. She just was. Her skin tone and black hair reminded Simone of Angel, who she was once again trying to forget. He was also an artist and unabashedly so. A slight smile crept across her face thinking of him despite her efforts not to. As she became mesmerized by Allie's presence, she couldn't shake the urge to speak his name, tell his story. Someone like Allie would love to know, to hear about that part of her life. Only Simone kept that part of herself hidden and would continue to do so for the next few decades if she could help it. That determination didn't stop his name from sliding across her lips. "Angel" she whispered under her breath as she stared down at her plate. Simone sipped some tea and met Allie's eyes again as she spoke of where'd she like to shoot in the morning.

"What time?" Simone asked. "I'd love to join you if you don't mind."

"Oh, nine I guess. Unless I have too many beers tonight, then ten." She said with a laugh.

"It's a date then."

"Are you guys coming over to the lounge tonight? It's a great spot to have a few drinks. God knows, there's nowhere else to go around here unless you want to drive a half hour." Jonah said. "Molly makes a mean highball, and the bartender is your classic Mainer, all grizzled around the edges."

"Sure, we'd love to. Right, Simone?" Ethan asked.

"Of course," Simone answered. If it involved listening to Allie's stories more, she was all in.

Simone settled onto a bar stool as another man fiddled with the jukebox. Simone watched him search for quarters.

"He's here every summer. Comes up from upstate New York. He and his wife used to vacation in Maine until she passed away when I was a kid. He still comes. As far as I know, he doesn't miss a summer. He plays Elvis. Never anything else." Molly said as she slid behind the bar and tied a white apron around her waist.

"That's sweet. I guess." Simone said as she spun around. She rubbed her fingers as Molly poured her some wine. Simone sipped. "A pinot noir?" She asked.

"Yep. You look like a pinot noir kind of girl." Molly winked at her.

"So, you can guess people's drinks by how they look or act?" Simone asked as she sipped.

"Yep. Been doing it since I was little. You grow up at a place like this, with strangers coming and going each week, week after week, summer after summer, you get a feel for folks." Molly said. She leaned her elbows on the bar. "While you are certainly a pinot noir woman today, I'm thinking there was a keg stand incident or two in college? Am I right?" Simone laughed and wiped the corner of her mouth.

"Don't we all have an incident or two in our past?" Simone said. Molly tapped her hand.

"Maybe by the end of the week, you'll have another incident to add to that list. This lounge can bring that out in a person. Trust me." Molly said.

"What about you? You've been here your whole life?"

"Nope, not at all. I spent my childhood here and then took off after college. Never planned to look back until my father died. I came back with my kid, who happens to be at her father's in Tennessee for a few more weeks. I was going to fix it up and sell, but I, well, I fell back in love with this place. I felt the need to stay, this time by my choosing." Molly said. "I didn't do much of my own choosing before that. Plus, you see that guy over there? The one who just came in? He kinda makes staying at Moose Pond Lodge a pretty good choice, too."

"That one? In the jeans? I saw him earlier outside when we got here, I think." Simone.

"Saw who, where?" Zack said as he ducked under the bar to get to Molly. He pinched her side and slid his hand out to Simone. "Zack Preston. You're the couple that came this afternoon? From Connecticut?" Simone blushed. He was rugged, like the help at her parents' house. But he was forward in a way they weren't. He looked her in the eye and squeezed her hand. His hands were strong like Ethan's but in a useful way.

"Hi, Zack. Yes, I'm Simone. My husband, Ethan, just ran to the cabin to get me a sweater. I didn't know Maine nights could get this chilly."

"We keep things hot in the lounge. Don't you worry." Zack said as he planted a kiss on top of Molly's head.

"Allie, Jonah. Let me get you started on something." Zack said as Allie and Jonah sat next to Simone. He cracked open two beers and slid them over. Allie swigged her beer and then looked at Simone as she sipped her wine.

"You definitely have to come with Molly and me hiking for spots for pictures tomorrow. I bet with your skin tone, build, and hair, I can get some incredible shots of you, too."

Simone stiffened her back and placed her wine glass on the bar. "Me? No, I haven't posed for photos in so many years. I'd feel ridiculous. Really." She swallowed.

"Now saying that is ridiculous. You're a natural beauty. I'm sure your modeling career was a crazy success." Allie said.

"It was. Don't let her fool you. She had magazine shoots in the Hamptons and NYC." Ethan said as he walked in and draped a sweater over her shoulders.

"Well, Ethan makes it sound more glamorous than it was."

"Bullshit. One of my favorite pictures of Simone is in front of Bethesda Fountain. You know, the famous fountain in Central Park? She looks like a dream. I have it on my desk." Ethan said as Zack nodded at a beer before sliding it over to him. Ethan sipped. "I found it at the bottom of a box of her college stuff when we moved into a larger house five years ago. It's my prize possession."

The word possession made Simone cringe. She pulled her sweater further over her shoulders. Simone sipped and closed her eyes for a moment. She thought about the day that picture was taken. Ethan never asked, and he certainly never asked why it was at the bottom of a box her parents had kept during that year she was gone. She felt a pit in her stomach remembering how her mother was convinced that box was all they'd ever have of her again. She also remembered the hours after that picture was taken. It was her first time alone with Angel. It was her first time doing anything she wasn't supposed to. Simone felt her cheeks get warm. Her palms sweated as she put down her wine glass and rubbed her fingers.

"You okay, Simone?" Molly asked from behind the bar.

"Oh yes. I guess just a little embarrassed, maybe." She said.

"Oh, no. I'm sorry to blather on. If you're uncomfortable posing for any pics, just say the word. I just never get to shoot people in nature, just bodies at crime scenes." Allie said as she took another big swig. Simone and Molly laughed.

"It's fine. I'll give it a try if you want." Simone said. She sipped some more.

"Great. All three of us will meet in the clearing after breakfast then? Molly, are you sure you can get away?" Allie asked.

"Hell yeah. I'm the boss, remember?" Molly said. Simone relaxed her shoulders. She envied Molly being her own boss. Simone had never been the boss of anything. Molly was short, much shorter than Simone, yet to Simone she seemed giant. She was loud, bouncy, alive. Molly exuded freedom and ease. Maybe, Simone thought, if she spent enough time around Molly and Allie, she'd feel a little at ease, free, exotic, confident, or at least alive.

After too many beers and too many stories about college football and prep school, Ethan hit the bed with a thud. By the time Simone emerged from the bathroom in a nightgown, he was snoring. She stood over him and watched. *He's a good man*, she thought. He was good to her in every way. He knew her past. He knew about that year, the missing persons' report, the rumors of drugs and white slavery. He even knew about the tattoo. Yet, he loved her enough to listen to the truth, trust in her, and help her walk with her head held high again. He essentially re-introduced Simone to the society that shunned her once it became public that she wasn't "taken" or held against her will. She wasn't a 90's version of the Hearst kidnapping. She slipped away with Angel, hid out in his Brooklyn studio apartment, and willingly spent an entire year pretending to be anyone but Simone Sterns-Forrester. They called her a 'spic-loving whore'. Despite the truth, the scandal of it all, Ethan Beckwith stepped forward with Simone on his arm and demanded everyone accepted her, accepted them. And, to Simone's surprise, they did. She owed it to him to not make him regret it, to not make a fool out of him. She owed it to their families, too. Until she got Angel's message in April, she had done a spectacular job upholding her end of the deal, being who they wanted and needed her to be.

Simone slipped on a sheer robe and stepped onto the tiny porch of Cabin 3. She melted into the rocking chair and let the night air settle over her long body. As the chair creaked, she leaned her head back and smiled. She was alone. The world was still and quiet. Simone couldn't remember the last time everything was that quiet. There was always noise in the house, at the showings, and the train into the city. The society meetings, luncheons, tennis matches, country club dinners, fundraisers, and business meetings were all filled with noise. She closed her eyes and rocked. She wanted more of the peace on the porch, more of the calm. Maybe, she thought, after two weeks in the woods of Maine, she'd find it.

The sunlight staggered through the white linen curtain above the bed. Simone peered one eye open to see morning wasn't just a dream. When she remembered she was meeting Molly and Allie early for a hike and pictures, she shot open both eyes and sat up. Ethan stirred next to her. He reached his arm across her lap as she scooted up to look at the time. He smiled up at her.

"Hey, lady. Sorry I fell asleep on you last night. Not the romantic adventure I had planned for our first night." He mumbled.

"It's okay. I sat on the porch, watched the stars. It was nice." Simone said as she patted his hand. She traced the outline of his fingers. She loved his hands.

"I even brought a bottle of your favorite champagne. Had it all planned. But, nope. I ruined it." He over-extended a frown. She giggled.

"Stop. It was fine. The wine at the lounge was fine, too. We can save the champagne for tonight. I'm going with the girls this morning. Remember?"

"Oh, yeah. To take pictures, right? I guess I'll head out in one of the canoes, do a little fishing." He mock-frowned again. Simone slid out from under his arm and laughed at him again.

After she showered, Simone stood in front of the mirror. She wiped the steam away and studied her face. She hadn't posed for actual pictures in ages. She used to love doing her makeup for shoots and runway shows. She loved the feel of a blow dryer working its magic on her fire red hair. She loved the softness of a good makeup brush wisping across her cheeks. Now, as she got ready for the day, she saw a few lines and freckles she never noticed in those days. She saw thinner lips, not as plump and bright pink as they had been. Even though she knew no one else really noticed those subtle signs, she did. Simone wished she could be one of those women who looked in the mirror and saw much more. She applied her standard high-end makeup, ran a massive round brush through her hair for volume, and practiced a smile to make sure she wasn't accentuating lines. Once she felt ready, prepared, she went to the porch and waited for the others. She was early, as usual.

Ethan handed her a bagel he brought back from the lodge and a travel mug filled with hot tea.

"Thank you, love. But I'm not eating this clump of white bread before I pose for pictures."

"More for me." He quipped as he scooped the bagel up from the side table. Ethan kissed her and headed through the door. "Have fun today. I love you." He shouted from outside. She leaned her head back. "Love you, too." She yelled. As she sipped, anxiety started to bubble up. Not only was she venturing into the woods for the second day in a row, but now she was going with two women she didn't know. Just as she started to ball up her fist and unclench her hands repeatedly, she spotted Allie exiting a cabin on the other side of the clearing. Allie was dressed in black jeans, a black tank top, and had a giant camera swaying across her chest. She glided across the clearing of wild daisies and black-eyed Susans. Allie's wide, white smile eased Simone's encroaching anxiety.

"Well, don't you just look like a dream in white and Caribbean blue," Allie said. She slid her sunglasses to the top of her head and rested her arm on the porch ledge.

"Thank you. And you, you look so, so glamorous, exotic. Black suits you."

"Thanks. I was never much for color. Except in my pictures, I guess." Allie said.

"Oh look. There's Molly. On the trail." Simone pointed, and Allie turned. Molly waved at them as she bounced their way.

"Ladies. It's a perfect day to get lost in the woods and snap some pics, don't ya think?" Molly shouted as she approached the clearing. "Come on this way. We'll hit the main trail to the pond then venture out further. Unless you have a better idea, Allie? You know the light and what's best."

"That sounds like a plan to me. The sun by the water will be perfect. Maybe get Simone here up on the rock for a pic?" Allie said.

"On a rock? Like in the middle of the water?" Simone asked as she walked behind Allie to meet Molly. Simone stumbled on a root and caught herself before Molly and Allie turned around. "How will I get out there?"

"Simple. Take off those boots and wade out. It's not deep at all. I'll walk out and help you climb up." Molly said. She glanced up and down at Simone. Simone was put at ease by her smile and confidence. "Trust me. You'll look like a dream on that rock. A black and white picture from behind? Will that look good, Allie?" Allie glanced back as she fiddled with her camera.

"I think shooting her at any angle, any light, in any medium will look incredible."

"Oh goodness. You give me too much credit. It's been a long time since I posed for anything or anyone."

"You're like a ballerina. Better yet, you remind me of the swans I take pictures of in the Public Garden in the city. They float by, long necks, pure white with complete and utter grace." Allie said. Simone raised her hand to her heart.

"Thank you for that."

"No, thank you for agreeing to do this," Allie said.

As they made their way down the path, Simone glanced around from the treetops to the trail. Suddenly, the woods didn't seem so intimidating or unknown. It was welcoming. The needle clusters on the sandy trail, the slight sway of greenery, and the silence were all soft. Simone could breathe easier. Her fingers relaxed. She unclasped her hands and let her long arms sway by her side as her eyes absorbed everything around her.

"I'm sorry you missed Emerson this time. She was so bummed her visit with her dad would coincide with you guys coming back." Molly said to Allie. "Don't get me wrong, she was anxious to get down there for a few weeks, but really wanted to see you guys again."

"Emerson? That's your daughter, right?" Simone asked as she tried to squeeze between Molly and the trail.

"Yep. She's there for six weeks. The longest visit yet. But, considering all the changes, she's adjusted quite well. I think." Molly said to Simone.

"So, if you don't mind me asking, how long have you been divorced?"

"Just a year. I came back last spring, fixed this place and ran it last summer. Then, decided to stay. I've only been back a little over a year. We were in the middle of the divorce when I came back here."

"That must've been tough. What, I mean, if you don't mind me asking..."

"What made me leave?" Molly asked as she looked down at the trail.

"Yeah, I mean, if...I'm sorry. I must sound nosey and rude." Simone looked down, too.

"No, not at all. It's okay. Well, long story short, I came back because my dad died. But I left my marriage because he was a lying, cheating asshat." The three women laughed. "In all seriousness, he cheated throughout the marriage. But it wasn't until I actually caught him, saw it with my own eyes, that I truly left. I kinda left before that, emotionally, but that was the last straw. It shouldn't have been. Honestly, I would've been better off leaving as soon as I knew there was anyone else, instead of waiting until there were lots of someone elses."

"That must've been hard, especially with a kid," Simone said. She folded her arms.

"Yeah, that certainly didn't make it easier. I'm fine now. Still a little angry, to be honest."

"Angry at him or the other women?" Allie asked. "I swear, I'd lose my mind if Jonah cheated."

"Both. I just don't get the cowardice of it, you know?" Molly looked forward. "Those women knew he was married with a kid and me at home. And, he knew I'd eventually find out. I wish he or one of them would've had the guts to step up and tell me sooner. I get that he didn't want to lose Emerson, but he could've let me go sooner, and I would've been okay."

"It's a respect thing, I think. You felt disrespected being in the dark, like a fool." Allie said.

"Exactly. That hurt more than realizing he didn't really love me. And those women, I mean seriously. What kind of woman runs around like that knowing she's hurting someone for no good reason?"

"Whores. Trashy-ass whores, Molly." Allie said. They laughed again.

"Yeah. You're right." Molly said as Allie nudged her with her elbow.

Simone had an ache in her chest. Her gut clenched. She squeezed her hands tight together. She thought of Ethan. Simone pictured the look on his face if he ever found out about her meeting Angel in April. It was one day, but one day that would devastate him and everyone else they knew. The idea that she was the other woman, unfaithful, a trashy-ass whore in the minds of anyone who found out, made her nauseous. Then, she pictured that afternoon with Angel being the last time she ever saw him, felt him. Simone gasped and drew her clenched fist to her heart. It raced.

"Hey, are you okay?" Molly asked. She placed her hand on Simone's shoulder. Simone couldn't stop several tears from surfacing. The pond came into view as the Molly took her arm and Allie stopped walking.

"Yes. I'm fine. I'll be just fine." Simone said as she stiffened her back and looked up at the sky. "I'm fine, ladies. Really." She bit her lip to stop it from quivering.

"Is it the idea of climbing on the rock? That was just a suggestion. You don't have to do anything you aren't comfortable with." Allie said. She rubbed Simone's shoulder.

"No, it's not that. I swear. The rock idea is fine. Mostly. It's just, well, I'm just feeling a little emotional about a few things, I guess, mistakes I've made." Simone shook her head and smoothed her hair behind her back. "I'm fine now. Shall I start to wade out to that rock?" Allie and Molly exchanged glances.

"Honey, we've all made mistakes. God knows I've chosen the hard way more times than I can count. I'm the most imperfect person I've ever known." Molly said with a laugh. "You wouldn't believe all the tears I've shed out here on this trail and in that pond, especially last summer. You go right ahead and get as emotional as you want, honey." Molly nodded at her. Simone smiled.

"Thank you, thank you both. I needed this break from my life. From all of it." Simone said. She reached down and unlaced her brand-new boots. She rolled up her white jeans to her knees. "Now, I'm going to walk to that rock, climb up, stare at those woods across the way, and figure my life out." Allie and Molly laughed.

"If it were that easy, I'd be living on that rock," Molly said. Simone smiled and slowly waded into the water. It was just as cold as the ocean at her beach house. She let the goosebumps climb up her legs, then arms. By the time she reached the rock, she couldn't feel her toes. Simone hoisted her skinny frame onto the rock and turned to face Allie and Molly. Allie was already on her knees leaning down for a shot.

"Go ahead and sit, face that way and pull your hair back. I think you'll love these once I get a few shots." Allie shouted. Simone sat and drew her knees up to her chest. The silence surrounded her tiny island. She thought of what Molly said about living on that rock. It seemed like a perfectly good idea suddenly. She wouldn't have to make any decisions. She wouldn't have to disappoint or hurt anyone, Ethan or Angel. Or, herself.

Simone could hear the clicks of Allie's camera. She wondered which version of herself, her life, was being documented for eternity. Was it the Simone from Greenwich who had everything so comfortable and clean? Or, was it the Simone who carelessly melted into the world of a poor street artist who softly licked her calf, knee, and up her thigh as they lay entangled in thread-bare sheets with nothing but stolen food to sustain them? Dammit, she thought to herself. She had everything with Ethan. Life was too easy, smooth. It was all she needed. They had a perfect life, a fulfilling existence. She did tons of good for charity. She beautified the historic homes of Greenwich. Her life with him mattered. Ethan mattered. He had done so much to ensure her lot in life, their life. He had also given up a lot. Ethan punched his college roommate when he found him circulating nude pictures that were taken by Angel for an exhibition, pictures that almost made the papers. Ethan saved her from herself and any semblance of a life wallowing in that studio with pennies and nothing more.

While Ethan stood firm and held her hand during the time she transitioned back into her old life, her parents needed more time. Her mother nearly vomited when she saw Simone at the police station and saw her tattoo. But, both parents swallowed their disgust, disgust for all that Angel wasn't, and embraced her even if they didn't mean it yet. Of course, they embellished the theory that Simone had some sort of a breakdown. There was no way they were going to let polite society know Simone loved every dirty and adventurous second of that year. They forced her to go along with that explanation. She eventually came to believe that's all it was, a dirty adventure, a breakdown.

Simone adjusted herself on the rock and flipped her hair to the side. She sighed and thought of that April afternoon where she almost fell back into that year. He still had that same studio. The smell of paint drying, leftover Chinese, and smoke. It smelled like him. Sensations of that year flooded her mind. They had made love every single day, repeatedly, wildly, all over the city. She remembered darting down alleys when cops came near them. Simone knew her picture was everywhere, on the news, in the papers. She chopped off her red hair and dyed it black to match Angel's. She was still white as a swan bobbing around the water. But with enough red lipstick, smudged eyeliner, and ripped tights peeking out from her denim shorts, she didn't resemble herself at all. She blended into his crowd, his entire existence. His friends, like him, were all undocumented and had no interest in telling the cops who she was, even with a hefty reward dangling. It was his immigration status that led her to walk back into her mother's arms at that police station. Her parents made it clear they'd have him deported before she could run back to his apartment. She'd never see him again regardless, that was until his message a few months ago.

Simone let her knees go and stretched her legs. She could still hear clicks. She straightened her back as Allie yelled out for her to turn her head slightly. She closed her eyes and thought of Angel touching her months ago in that same bed. It was a blur, and the hours seemed like days. She remembered the feeling of his sweaty black hair falling on her shoulders as he climbed on top of her. No, she thought. She couldn't be that Simone again, not for a day, a week, or certainly not for years. An afternoon on a whim was more than enough. It was too much. She was Ethan's Simone. That's who she wanted to be and vowed to be. She'd have to carry that afternoon tucked in the corner of her heart forever--never to see the light of day again. Simone decided on that rock alone in the middle of the pond that she'd spend the rest of her life making sure Ethan never knew about those hours. No one would ever know.

"Simone?" Allie shouted. "Are you in another world?" She shook her head and turned to face them. "We've been shouting your name. Where were you?"

Simone slid off the rock and back into the knee-deep water. "Nowhere. I was nowhere." She muttered as she waded back to the sandy shore. Her heart ached again. Angel, his apartment, his sheets, his hands and mouth on her would stay hidden, unseen and unfelt. It would be a faded scar no one else could see, just like where his name once was. "I'm right here now." She said. "I'm here."

After they walked back to the clearing, Simone excused herself from Allie and Molly. She decided a nice nap in the hammock behind the cabin sounded like heaven.

"Thank you, guys, so much for today. I loved being out there. It really cleared my head." Simone said.

"I'll show you the pictures after dinner tonight? I think you'll love them. Ethan might want to buy a few." Allie said.

"He might. I'm sure they're lovely. I'll see you ladies tonight." Simone said as she backed away.

"Lobster tonight. Don't be late. Zack makes incredible grilled corn on the cob." Molly shouted as Simone disappeared behind cabin 3.

"Great. I love lobster. See you gals then." She said back as their voices faded.

Simone gingerly sunk into the hammock tied between two pines. She pulled her phone from her back pocket. There were three messages. She swallowed. She didn't need to open them to know they were from Angel. She swiped. Three texts from "Marie," the name under which she saved Angel's information. She meant to delete it, block it altogether, but there was never a perfect moment. Simone started to shake. She clicked on the messages. She couldn't catch her breath.

"You can't just ignore me or what happened between us. What we both feel, always felt."

"I don't want to cause you any trouble, mi alma."

"Tell me you don't love me and I'll fade away again. Mi Vida. I need you to say it."

Simone drew the phone to her chest. Her heart was beating with a painful thud. *Delete them*, she thought. The words 'mi alma' created a lump in her throat. My soul, that's what he always called her. Simone lifted the phone in front of her as she swayed on the hammock. She texted him.

"I was bored. I'm sorry." She hit send and instantly wanted to reach into the phone and delete the words. No, no, no, she whispered. Her eyes darted around. Her fingers lingered over her phone. She fought back a river of tears just picturing his face reading those words. Just as she closed her eyes and let out a faint wail, she heard a ding.

"Bullshit, Mi Alma. Bullshit. You've been fucking bored for years with him. You were awake with me. Alive. Leave me forever to die with a broken heart, but don't lie to me and say that's the only reason you came to our city. I know your heart and every inch of your body. I am your soul. You are mine."

Simone reread Angel's text over and over. Her eyes kept falling onto the words 'awake' and 'I am your soul.' She held the phone close and stifled another wail. That afternoon swirled in her mind, again. They had made love against the door as soon as he unlocked it. They made their way to the bed and drank wine as they meshed into one another. He slid his hand along her thigh and hip, up to her chest, as he kissed her shoulder. She ran her hands through his hair. She missed that hair and his smell. He engulfed her neckline in kisses and grabbed her hip harder. Before she could put her wine glass down, he had slid her further down on the bed, and they were making love again. Her hair was wet with spilled wine on the sheet. There was no world outside of that apartment. There was nothing but his touch, his body melting into hers. Simone was lost in his world again. She tingled all over afterward. He never stopped kissing her shoulders, neck, hands, and hip. There was no time, no beginning or end to the day. Even though twenty years had passed since he was inside of her, everything about him was familiar, was home.

Then, her phone dinged on the floor. Time mattered again. The world outside mattered again and sucked away her attention from his soft mouth on hers. She remembered the panic she felt gathering her clothes from the floor after the real world crept back into his apartment. Simone closed her eyes again. She had slid her underwear and dress on so quickly, she nearly forgot her bra. She needed to catch the train to be home before Ethan. His driver was known for getting him home quickly on Saturdays.

She let the hammock sway as she remembered the way Angel grabbed her arm and asked her to stay. He was naked, and his muscles bulged throughout his body. He couldn't let go or take his eyes off hers. She darted her eyes away and cried. He released his grip. He slid his hand down to her hip and leaned in. "I'm still there." He whispered as his hands touched her scar through her dress. She nodded.

"I know." She whispered back to him. He kissed her earlobe then stepped back. Simone forced her feet to move forward and not look back. She was ripping out her own heart, and his, too. His breath behind her quickened. She knew he wanted to reach out and grab her again, throw her down and make love all over again. She knew it took everything he had inside not to force her to stay. As she opened the door and stepped out, she hoped he knew it took everything she had not to let him.

Simone stopped the tears and looked at her phone again. She ran her fingers over his words once more. She pressed the back button. Simone deleted his messages. She needed to delete him once more. That afternoon, just as that year, had to stay in that apartment. She had to leave it behind. The hammock swayed more. She felt sick to her stomach. She turned off her phone, scared he'd send another text and just as scared he never would again. "Angel," she whispered into the air. "I'm so sorry. I can't." She closed her eyes again and let her phone slide down to her side.

Simone drifted off into a much-needed nap as she listened to nearby willow branches rustle. Streaks of sun crossed her face and through her eyelids. She appreciated the intermittent warmth as she let silence and the breeze lull her to sleep. After a good nap, she told herself, everything would be fine. Life would fall back into place. Ethan would be back from fishing. They'd change, go off to dinner, sip wine, make love, and drift off to sleep. Their days would be refined, reliable, smooth, and comfortable. She was blessed to have him, she told herself. Simone just needed to keep that afternoon where it belonged. She needed to keep everything about Angel where it belonged, far from the light of day.

Chapter 3

Molly

Molly headed back to the main lodge after leaving Simone at her cabin and Allie to wander the trails for more pictures. As she reached the bridge, she could hear the water from the creek rush over the rocks. Molly stopped to watch for a moment. That creek had meandered its way around the scattered stones for decades, even longer. She used to watch it as a kid and could never figure out how it didn't change direction or paths. She assumed it was free to go around the other side of rocks or cut a little deeper into the sides. Sometimes, after a harsh enough winter, it did carve out a little more for itself. It expanded its borders, rushed over stones rather than appease the power of the rocks in its way. Molly leaned down and watched a cluster of needles race from rock to rock, only to get caught up in the rush of water and be taken to its destination without a say. Molly continued across the bridge and back to the lodge. Unlike those needles and that ever-flowing stream, she had a say, and for the first time in a long time, she was content with what the destination looked like. Molly thought of her birthday wish, for nothing to change.

As she rounded the last curve of the trail and the lodge came into view, she heard hammering.

"What is he up to now?" Molly said.

Zack was on the steps of the gazebo with a notebook sitting beside him. Molly crept up behind and waited for one more pound of a loose nail.

"Boo!" She yelled as she grabbed his shoulder. Zack swung around and grabbed her belt loop. He pulled her down to the step next to him.

"What are you trying to do? Make me hammer my damn hand to this gazebo?" Zack said as Molly leaned over and kissed his cheek. She laughed. "So, pictures are done, huh?"

"Yeah. It was fun. Simone is very interesting. Kinda a mystery, I think."

"A mystery, huh?" Zack said. He picked up the notebook. "Come on, you and I've known women like that and families like that. Seems a bit too un-mysterious. Very vanilla, plain, formal, stick-up-the-ass, as they say. You know?"

"Nah. Normally, I might agree with you. But, there's something there, more than what's on the surface with those brand-new boots and fear of anything woodsy. I think there's a story there, honey. She's got some dirt hidden away. I can feel it." Molly said.

"How about Allie? They seem pretty happy still." Zack said as he hammered one more nail.

"Yeah. A little quiet. And dressed all in black again today. With as hot as it is, just seems kinda odd. I dunno."

She leaned her head on his shoulder to get a look at the notebook. "What's all this?"

"Well, something I wanna talk to you about. I want to build on a little. Maybe expand the bedrooms, maybe build another one on?" Zack said as he took a pencil from behind his ear.

"Expand the bedrooms? What for? You mean like the guest rooms? We keep the ones I've got filled, but I don't think we need to add more. I mean, business is good, but not *that* good."

"I don't mean for the guests. I mean for us, me, you, Em, and a room for Hannah." Zack said as Molly stood up straight.

"Hannah has a room at your place. You want to add on for when she stays here now and then?"

"That's just it, Molly. I don't want to have a place anymore. I mean really, I stay out here more often than not already. Why pay the mortgage on a house I barely live in, especially this spring and summer? C'mon, don't you think it just makes sense if I move in? I can handle most of an addition myself." Zack said. He reached over and took Molly's hand.

"Move in?" Molly said. She stepped back.

"Well, damn. Don't make it sound so awful. Seriously, I practically live here now. And you know Em would love it. Hannah loves you and Em. It would be an easy transition for her."

"I didn't mean for it to sound like that," Molly said. She reached for his hand. "I just, I like the way things are right now, between us. I guess I don't see the need to go changing everything."

Zack stepped back and stretched his arms over his head. He put his hands on his hips and stepped down onto the grass. "I've been hunched over all day pounding in loose nails." He said. "Listen, is this because of last summer? Are you afraid to let me move in? Be honest, honey. I mean, I think we're past all that. We've got a great thing here, and I just assumed you'd be ready to take it to the next level like I am."

Molly walked over to him. "No, it's not about last summer. I don't see the need to change anything. If it ain't broke, don't fix it. Right? Isn't that what you always say about stuff here? Huh?"

Zack laughed. "Yeah, that's what I say, smartass. But, that's about this place, not us. We ain't broke. We don't need fixing. But, I think we need to move forward. I'm ready. I've been ready since I drove back here that day last July. I knew the second I got out of my truck and walked over to you that you're all I want. I want this for the long haul, Molly. I know it's taken you a little longer, and you were a little gun shy when I came back, but dammit. I think we're past that." He reached for her beltloop again. She looked up at him.

"Why does the long haul have to be any different than what we have now? I mean seriously. This works. Me and you, here working together all day, having some fun at night when Em's gone. This here, this path we're on, it's all good. If you move in, what happens if it becomes, I dunno, not so good?" Zack pulled back a little. "Don't, don't pull back. I'm serious. Wouldn't it hurt the kids if we did this move in together thing and then something happened?"

"Don't use the kids as an excuse. It's you, Molly. It's still you being afraid something will happen."

"Do you blame me?" Molly said. She looked down at her feet.

"So, we're back to that, huh? What else do I have to do to prove to you that this is what I want?" Zack stepped back. The space between them grew even more.

"Nothing, Zack. I don't need you to do anything."

"That's it right there, Molly Watts. You don't need me. You don't need anyone, do you?" Zack said. He turned and walked away. Molly drew in a deep breath. She opened her lips to call his name, ask him to stop. But, nothing came out. She watched him walk away to the porch of the main lodge. He ascended the steps and disappeared inside. Molly walked over the steps of the gazebo and picked up his hammer and notebook. She sat inside the gazebo and looked at his sketches. Molly sighed. "Well, Zack Preston. This would make a nice addition." She tilted her head back and exhaled loudly. "Nope. It ain't broke." She said.

Molly let her mind wander back to last summer when he reappeared after breaking up with her. She told him then she'd only give it another shot if they took things slow this time, kept it casual. Molly couldn't dive back in, head first, and get hurt like that again. She practically drowned in her lust and love for him. She couldn't handle that again. She demanded they make a pact to keep it light. Molly didn't need the distraction now that she decided to keep the lodge. Emerson and Moose Pond Lodge would come first. He could come after all that. He agreed. They went on a few traditional 'dates' in town. They took Emerson and Hannah to the beach once Hannah's legs healed enough from the car accident. They all four went apple picking in the fall. He came by on Thanksgiving and ate, then stayed the night after Emerson went to bed. Christmas was nothing but making love all over the lodge because Emerson was in Tennessee with her father. They spent New Year's Eve hosting a party at the lodge. Maxine, her best friend, and her family, Zack's family, and everyone who ever worked at the lodge stayed. Molly had one glass of champagne, her first drink in months. She relished in the company and feeling of closeness and community. Her first holiday season back in Maine was everything she could ask for. She felt like she belonged, and not just in the capacity of running the resort but being a part of the community. Molly wasn't just home, she felt at home. She kissed Zack at midnight. As he held her hips and lifted her off the ground, Molly knew the coming year would be more than she could've imagined when she pulled back into Moose Pond Lodge months beforehand. She wanted to stay in that moment, that moment of light and weightlessness. Everything was rolling along as it was supposed to. The path she was on, like the water cascading along the rocks, was going in the exact direction she wanted, and nothing would change it.

"Why do you want to go changing things now, Zack?" Molly said into the air as she ran her fingers along his design.

As Molly and Zack prepared the dinner for the guests, they stayed arms-length apart. They exchanged cordial directions, questions, and 'could you pass me the—' requests typical of their lodge dinners. Molly told herself to let their words that afternoon fade into the background. She didn't want to discuss the idea any further. She certainly didn't want to fight with him, something she had never had a reason to do since he pulled back into the resort. As Molly took the large metal tongs to the water to fish out another lobster, she twisted her mouth as the hot steam settled on her face. Maybe a good fight was what they needed? She thought. Maybe if he saw upending everything would create unnecessary conflict, he'd say forget it. Zack reached over the pot to grab the large container of sea salt. He grunted. She knew that grunt. It meant he was frustrated. He did it anytime there was a problem he couldn't instantly fix.

"How long are you gonna stay pissed at me, anyway?" She said as she flinched from the steam.

"I'm not pissed." He said as she sprinkled salt. "I'm just surprised. I thought you'd be excited. I thought, well, I thought you wanted what I wanted. I thought this whole 'casual' talk was just, well, talk." He said. "I gotta get these out back if they are gonna be ready in time." Zack walked out the back door with a tray filled with corn on the cob.

"Zack, I'm just finally in a good place. We're in a good place." Molly yelled out to him as he pushed the door open.

"So that means we can never get to a better place? Is that what you're saying? Keep the status quo forever? Jeez, Molly. I get you needed to step back from everything and practice a little moderation, between the drinking and everything else. But really? You gonna take everything in life in moderation now?" He said as the door closed behind him.

Molly stepped back from the pot and checked her watch. It was time to pull three lobsters out and add three more. She removed the red bodies as steam rose above them. Molly took the kitchen shears and snipped the bands off the rest of the lobsters. She gently picked up one at a time and lowered them into the roaring water. She always cringed when there was a hiss as the boiling water swallowed them. Within seconds, they had gone from clueless critters wandering around a tank, then box, to a delicacy for tourists looking for an authentic taste of Maine. There was no moderation when serving up her weekly lobster feast to visitors. It was always a spectacular show for the tourists—too many lobsters followed by too much blueberry pie.

But Zack was right, she thought. She had spent the last year carefully moderating everything in her own life. Molly needed to. The idea of losing control, falling back into the habit of drinking away the nights in the lounge every time something didn't go as she expected, and ignoring the needs of her daughter at the same time, was all too much to risk again. If it took careful, mindful moderation of every aspect of her life to keep herself steady, then that's what she was going to do, whether Zack liked it or not. She had successfully kept her bourbon habit in check. She poured herself into the task of making life as calm and routine as possible for Emerson. She even got to a point where she was friendly with Kenny the Philanderer in a genuine way. What Molly and Zack had was fun, playful, and dependable. She didn't need him to unnecessarily stir the pot, stoke the embers of her impulse control. She needed him to stay the way he was, the way they were together. She hated to admit it to herself as she fished out the last lobster. He was right about being scared. If she let him in any further, if she let him in entirely, losing him again would be unbearable. Despite getting to know his ex, Hannah's mom, Melissa, a little better throughout the year, Molly couldn't help but be a bit gun shy. She still harbored a smidge of resentment over how easily Zack walked away from her last July. Just 48 hours alone with Melissa dealing with a horrible scare with their child was all it took for Zack to walk away once. While she didn't fear Melissa wanted him back or he wanted her back in any way, she begrudgingly feared unpredictable circumstances might create another perfect storm that could upend their causal, easy life together. She didn't want to risk playing house if one vicious storm could make it crumble, leaving her alone to pick up the pieces.

At dinner, Molly sat across from Allie and Jonah, far from Zack. He kept shooting her glances as she immersed herself in conversations about daily life in the city, especially funny stories of trying to save parking spots on the street during the back-to-back nor'easters. Her first winter back in Maine had been an eye-opening experience after 15 years in Nashville. Molly didn't realize how much she missed and loathed snow at the same time. Without Zack plowing her out, helping her shovel, and basically being a one-man snow rescue patrol, she didn't know how she would've made it. As she told Allie and Jonah about his help as she eased herself back into the ruggedness of a Maine winter, she saw Zack looking at her.

"What? You know I'm grateful for all you do. Don't look at me that way." Molly shouted to his table. Zack got up and picked up the tray of corn on the cob. He walked behind Molly and placed one on her plate. "Thank you." She said. He kissed the top of her head and walked to the other side.

"Well, next winter, I might be too busy to come all the way out here to rescue your stuck ass from that ditch across the road," Zack said as he pulled up a chair next to Allie. "So, Allie and Jonah, when did you two decide it was the right time to move in together?"

"Well, I would've moved in with him the first night," Allie said with a laugh. "His place was so much nicer than mine and closer to the paper."

"Yeah, there was no way we were moving to her crappy apartment. Plus, she had the most obnoxious roommate. What was her name? Glory or something?"

"Liberty. Her name was Liberty. She wasn't that bad. I couldn't be too picky once I got dumped by my last boyfriend and couldn't afford a place on my own. I kinda had like two weeks to find something. It wasn't that bad. But his was definitely better. Plus, he was a good cook."

Jonah took Allie's hand and kissed it. "Yeah, she would've lived under a bridge and ate scraps from Quincy Market if I hadn't have let her move in when I did."

"I'm serious. Really, when did you know? See, I've been with this chick for a year. I work at her place. I'm there all the time. I stay the night at least twice a week, oh and she's totally hot. I want to sell my place. It's too big for just me, and I'm hardly ever there. But, this chick says it's too soon." Zack said as he rested his chin on his palm and winked at Molly.

"I never said it's too soon," Molly said as she wiped corn off her mouth. "I said why change things up when what we've got is working out great?"

Allie and Jonah exchanged glances. Allie's eyes widened. "Well, I think it depends on *how* hot she is. Right, Jonah?" She shot Molly a wink and Jonah laughed.

"Funny. But seriously, they're here for their first anniversary, and you want to drag them into this?" Molly said to Zack.

"What? I'm not dragging them into anything. I'm seeking guidance about relationships from a happily married couple."

"Oh, it's fine. Drag me in. I'll throw my opinion around whether you ask or not." Allie said. "So, what's the true hold up, Molly? If he's here all the time anyway, what's the difference?"

"Well, it's just a lot of change, I guess. I'm happy, content, with the way things are. Aren't you Zack?" Molly asked.

"Of course. I'm happy the way things are, too. But I think we could be happier if we made it more permanent. What's wrong with that? I swear, Molly Watts, you might be the only woman I've ever met who doesn't want to take a relationship to the next level. You want to keep things casual. Well, maybe I'm done with casual." Zack said.

"I don't think we need to discuss this in front of everyone. Do you?" Molly said. She wiped her hands and took a sip of tea. She shot Zack a look she knew would make her point. He smiled at her and winked again. Simone and Ethan entered the dining room. Molly stood to greet them as Zack reached for two more chairs for the table.

"Hi, guys. You're just in time to stick your noses in Molly and Zack's relationship." Allie shouted out to them. Molly shot the same look. Ethan laughed and shook Zack's hand.

"Hey, I'm all for sticking my nose in. What's the issue at hand?" Ethan said.

Before Molly could get back to her seat, Zack, Allie, and Jonah were filling in the details. She couldn't help but smile listening to Zack's dramatization of her not wanting to move in together. Allie egged it on by asking if Molly was waiting for a hotter landscaper/cook/carpenter/plow guy/fireplace starter to come along. Simone was laughing before she could get her sweater off.

"You guys are a cute couple. And, you're obviously in love. So, I vote you move in together." Simone said as she poured some tea.

"Well then. It's unanimous. I will put my place on the market tomorrow." Zack said as he threw his fist in the air to declare victory. He raised his eyebrows at Molly. She laughed.

"Not so fast, big guy. We still have lots to talk about before anyone sells anything. And, this isn't the time or place to do it."

"She sounds serious, buddy. I'd hold off on the victory dance." Jonah said. "But, still put your place on the market anyways." He winked at Zack.

Molly shook her head as she finished her dinner.

Afterward, they all headed to the lounge for drinks. As Molly said 'hi' to Carl, she climbed behind the bar to tie an apron. Allie slid onto a barstool. Simone sat next to her.

"Thanks again for today. It felt good to sit on the rock alone, walk through the woods, and all. I don't get enough of that kind of experience. Well, if I'm being honest, I don't ever get that kind of experience."

"No, don't thank me. I should thank you. Jonah is getting my camera so I can show you some pictures. Shooting you on that rock was awesome. I think you'll love them." Allie sipped a beer Molly slid over to her. "So, you don't get to enjoy the outdoors much in Greenwich?"

"We do have a beach house in the Hamptons. So, there's that. I get plenty of beach time. But woods, well, that's a different story." Simone said as Molly poured her wine and rested her elbows on the bar to lean into them.

"She's not lying about the pictures. They turned out great. I gotta tell you. You looked very natural on that rock." Molly said.

"I'm going outside to watch the sunset. Alright, honey?" Ethan said to Simone. She nodded as he kissed her cheek.

"I'll join you," Zack said as he grabbed a beer. He pinched Molly's side. "Since I'm staying here tonight, I can have a few beers with the guys. That is if I'm off duty, ma'am."

"Get out," Molly said. Just as the guys walked out, Jonah ducked in with the camera.

"Here ya go. I'm gonna go out with those guys." Jonah said as he took a beer from Molly's hand. The screen door slammed shut. Allie started her camera and pulled up Simone's pictures on the screen.

"Here. Press that button to go forward and touch this to zoom in. I'm thinking black and white for most. But, if you see ones you want in color, I'll gladly get them for you and Ethan."

Simone put down her glass and took the camera. Molly leaned over the bar to look even though she had seen most of them earlier. Simone's red hair fell over her shoulders as she looked down to scroll through the pictures. She stopped mid-way through and looked up at Allie and Molly.

"What? You don't like them?" Allie said. She placed her hand on Simone's arm. Molly shrugged her shoulders as she looked at Allie.

"No, no. It's not that at all. I love them. They remind me of what I used to look like. I think. Or, used to be like, I guess. They remind me of pictures a friend took years ago." Simone looked at Molly and teared up.

"Hey, don't cry. There's no crying in my lounge." Molly said as she grabbed a bar napkin and handed it to Simone. Simone dabbed her eyes and flashed a half-smile Molly's way.

"I'm sorry. I don't know where this is coming from. I'm completely out of my element here, everywhere lately. And, oddly enough, I don't want to go back. I'm, well, I guess I'm just a bit of a mess lately. A mess and I don't know how to pretend I'm not anymore."

"Oh my. We're all messes at times. You should've seen me last year. I cried in here nearly every night. Almost every damn night. I had no idea where I was going, what I wanted, anything. My divorce was in full gear. My dad died here. I was screwing up with my kid big time. I was as lost as lost could be. I was drinking myself into oblivion over it all. I was beyond a bit of a mess." Molly said. She patted Simone's other arm from across the bar. "But, your guy, Ethan. Things are good there, right? You seem in love. He seems like the kind of guy who could help his girl feel better."

"Oh, yes. He's wonderful. I don't know what I'd do without him. But..." Simone leaned down and started to whisper. "I've had some issues from my past recently crop up. Issues he doesn't know about. Can't know about."

Molly leaned in further. She thought back to her conversation with Zack. She knew Simone had a story and her heart quickened at the thought that this story was about to come out of Simone's mouth. "What do you mean issues?" she asked. Allie's eyes widened. She shot Molly a quick glance telling Molly she was equally curious.

"A person. Someone I loved. God, did I love him. He's reached out, and it's got me all so confused. I've felt dizzy since the night I got his very first message. I'm sorry. I shouldn't even be talking about any of this. It would kill Ethan if he knew. You have no idea what that man has done for me." Simone wiped her eyes again. Her hand started to shake as she drew her wine glass to her lips.

"Well, take my advice, Simone. If you've got a good thing with Ethan, keep it. Don't make any more contact with this guy or see him. Nothing good will come of it." Molly said. She darted her eyes around to be sure the guys weren't coming back in.

"It's too late." Simone sighed. Allie tapped her arm.

"Oh, honey. Sounds like you need time to figure out what you want. Time alone, maybe? Would this guy be worth it, though? Losing what you have now?" Allie asked.

"Time alone, Allie? She needs to either stop with the guy from the past or leave Ethan. You can't condone keeping this guy on the side while she decides. That's not right to do to her husband." Molly said.

"All I'm saying is that maybe she needs time away to decide what to do," Allie said. She shrugged her shoulders. "What's wrong with that?"

"I have no idea what to do," Simone said as she looked down at her hands in her lap. Simone twisted her fingers in a knot.

"Well, speaking as someone who was cheated on constantly during my marriage, I'd say there's a whole hell of a lot wrong with the whole situation." Molly stood straight up behind the bar and crossed her arms. She knew her cheeks were getting red. "No offense, Simone. I don't know your situation. But, trust me, going outside of your marriage isn't going to fix anything, especially if you think there's a chance you want to stay with your husband."

"Molly, that's not fair. Your situation was totally different. Your husband was a serial cheater." Allie said. She took Simone's hand. "I don't think Simone is remotely like that."

"No, no I'm not. It's a complicated story. I'm not some two-bit whore who takes adultery lightly." Simone looked around again and lowered her voice even more.

"Listen. I'm not saying that. All I'm saying is cheating is cheating. And, well, there are real repercussions. People get hurt. Whether it's once or a hundred times, it's excruciating to get over. I felt horrible about myself." Molly felt tears well up in her eyes. "Regardless of the reason, it leaves scars. As much as I trust Zack and have moved on, it still hurts to think what a fool I was. Everyone but me knew, and that's an awful feeling." She wiped a tear with the back of her hand. "There's never a good reason to cheat, to be the other woman, to break up a family. Never." Molly swallowed a lump in her throat. She looked over Simone's shoulder to see an older man at the jukebox staring straight at her. His eyes went through her.

"I'm sorry for what happened to you, Molly. I am. I didn't mean to upset you. I just needed to let some of it out." Simone said. Allie rubbed her shoulder.

"No, Simone. I'm sorry. It's just a touchy subject. I didn't mean to make you feel bad or anything. I've just got strong feelings about this subject. That's all." Molly reached out to tap Simone's hand when she saw the man's gaze still fixed on her. "Can I help you?" She said over Simone to the man. He shook his head and turned his back to her.

"How about we change the subject. Sex? Anyone want to talk about sex? The fun kind, not this heavy stuff?" Allie asked. She sipped her beer as Simone and Molly laughed. Molly refilled their drinks but kept one eye on the man. She had seen him a few times in town, but never at the lounge. It wasn't unusual for a local to show up on the weekends and have a few drinks with the tourists. However, she usually knew something about them. Molly couldn't help but notice this man had an uneasy aura. He seemed out of place. He wasn't interacting with any of the other locals who sat at the opposite end of the bar talking to Carl. He was tall, gangly almost. Molly thought he had a 'weathered' look to him. He had deep wrinkles, a roadmap from his forehead to his chin. She was both curious about his story, but at the same time, uneasy about him. Molly flashed a faint smile when he looked up at her again. He didn't return the gesture but turned around to face the jukebox. Molly shrugged her shoulders and focused on Simone and Allie giggling.

"What's so funny?" Molly leaned back down on the bar in front of them. "I wasn't paying attention."

"Oh. I was telling Simone about my first time. It was after a football game, and, well, let's just say I didn't realize until afterward we were being watched by a group of junior high kids. I'm just glad there weren't phones back then if you know what I mean." Allie gulped her beer. "Can I get another, bartender, before the big guy drags me away for the night."

"Sure thing," Molly said as she laughed and opened another bottle. "Simone? More pinot?" Simone nodded. Molly poured her another glass and leaned in further close to her face. "Hey, listen. I'm sorry about earlier. I just get a little touchy about what happened in my marriage. You do what's right for you. Okay?"

"I wish I knew what that was, Molly. I honestly do." Simone said. She drew her glass to her lips. Molly shrugged her shoulders.

"Well, while you're here, I'm here to listen. No judgment. I promise."

"Thank you," Simone said. Molly nodded toward the door. The guys were coming in. Zack winked at her as he made his way to the bar. Molly's heart fluttered as it always did when he threw a wink her way. He nudged her side when he made his way to her. Zack leaned down and kissed the top of her head as he slid his finger through her belt loop. A year ago, she thought she lost him. She was floundering, thinking of selling the resort, and feverishly trying to repair her friendship with her best friend and her daughter. When Zack walked back across her driveway during Allie and Jonah's reception, everything in her relaxed, her mind, her gut, her muscles. Even before hearing him explain or apologize, she knew he'd fix what broke between them just by being there. Molly knew she still had work to do on herself, her relationship with Maxine and Emerson, but she was fully capable of doing the hard work needed. She was taking steps forward each day by controlling her reliance on alcohol to deal with any unexpected crisis, or just deal in general. She didn't feel her mouth water every time she walked past those bottles of bourbon. With or without Zack back in her life, she had a handle on things. But, having him there was a nice cushion to make it all easier. While taking the next step was natural, Molly still liked the idea that he was just a cushion to ease any fall, not a savior to keep her from falling. If he moved in, if things progressed too far, there'd be no turning back. While she needed him, loved him, and couldn't imagine a day without him, she didn't want to need or love him too much. She still wanted to stand on her own and feel confident that whether he came or went, nothing would knock her down that far again.

As the couples filtered out of the lounge, hand in hand, tipsy and giddy with love, or the illusion of love, Molly watched Simone closer. She noticed her fidgeting, her uneasiness with herself. Simone's words echoed in Molly's head, 'out of my element.' Molly wanted to embrace her and tell her to stay there forever. Moose Pond Lodge could help anyone find their 'element', their place, themselves.

Once the lounge was clean, and Carl hung up his apron to disappear into the night, Zack locked the doors. He always double checked the locks, even on nights he wasn't staying. He raised his eyebrows at her as she flung a wet bar towel over the shiny wood bar that looked as freshly cut as the day her father installed it 30 years ago. He motioned for her to come closer. She smiled and ducked under the bar to get to him. Zack grabbed her belt loops and pulled her tight against him. He leaned down and kissed her hard and long. He pulled back just as she got dizzy.

"Let's get down the hall to that bed, lady." He said. She swayed a little as he led her down the hall into the darkened bedroom. He swooped her up and kicked the door closed with his foot as he walked her to the edge of the bed. Zack slid Molly down slowly until her feet brushed the floor. He reached down and slid her shirt over her head. She untied her hair and shook her head. He ran his hand from the top of her jeans up her side and to her chest. His fingers barely made contact as he slid them slowly upward to her chin. With both hands, he lifted her chin towards his mouth. Molly looked up at him as the moonlight bounced off the wall and his shoulders. She loved full moons in Maine. She could see every detail of his face and lock of hair as he leaned down to kiss her. He leaned her back on the bed as she moaned. She scooted up. He unbuttoned her jeans and slid them off as she moved towards the pillows. Then he slid off his jeans and pulled his shirt over his head. Zack crawled over top of her and kissed her harder. He laid on his side and pulled her over his way. Before she could move her hair from her face, he lifted her on top of him.

"Sit up, honey," He whispered as he released her from his grasp. "I want to look at you." She smiled and giggled for a moment. "I'd die a happy and complete man if I took my last breath looking up at you like this." Her smile grew wide.

"You're quite the charmer there," She whispered as she leaned down to kiss him. He pressed his hand to her belly and placed the other on her hip.

"I'm serious, Mol. You're the most beautiful sight I've ever seen." He pulled her down to him. Zack grabbed her hips and pressed her body down hard. He ran his hand through her hair as they made love. Molly felt the sweat between them seal their bodies together as one. His breath on her ear and slight nibble on her shoulder sent her into another world. Nothing else existed but him and her in the moonlight filling the room. His scent, his moans, were all-encompassing. Her sense of balance, moderation, and control all went out the window when they made love. Afterward, it always took her a while to get her equilibrium back. As Molly drifted off to sleep with nothing but corners of a sheet covering their intertwined legs, Zack kissed her forehead again.

"This, Molly. I want this every night." He whispered in the dark. "Just think about it." She smiled and ran her hand up his chest. "I will. I promise." As she danced in between sleep and the last seconds of being awake, Molly wondered if it could really be this way forever. Could they suspend themselves in ecstasy and never touch the ground? Do people have this and keep it forever, like she was sure her parents would've if her mother hadn't passed away? Was it possible to be this happy and content and *stay* that way? Then, she wondered if it was worth the risk of finding out. Maybe it was.

Between full cabins and constant texting with Emerson to make sure she was enjoying her time in Nashville, the days were blending into each other. Molly was relieved to see Allie and Simone wandering the hiking trails. She remembered it was Allie's not so subtle wisdom last summer that helped Molly feel secure in her ability to run the resort and her decision to stay. While Molly still had moments of regret for not returning to see her dad or taking more significant steps to repair their relationship, she didn't immerse herself in the memories of his alcoholic days and nights. Molly didn't let his vices become her own. She didn't let the arguments, the resentment, of the past fill the lodge anymore. Molly had spent the better part of a year replacing those memories with new ones of her and Zack, Emerson and Hannah, loving and living in the lodge. If she didn't meet Allie when she did, Molly wasn't sure she'd have any of it or the peace of mind that came with it.

Another perfectly sunny and warm summer day in Maine faded to night. Emerson was due to fly home in one more week. Molly appreciated being busier than usual. As she helped finish cleaning the dining room and kitchen, Molly could hear the lounge coming to life. Music was turned up. The laughter rolled from the lounge and around the stone fireplace. She paused as she rung out a dish rag. Molly smiled. She knew her parents would love to see the resort brought back to life. She could almost hear her mother laugh as a memory of her father spinning her mom around came to mind. Molly followed the sounds of happiness to the lounge.

"Hey, Molly. Where's Zack? Thought I saw him leave after dinner." Jonah said from a barstool next to Allie.

"Yeah, he went home tonight. He gets Hannah, his daughter, tomorrow bright and early. He'll be back out tomorrow after lunch sometime. I think he plans to take her fishing." Molly said. She tied an apron. "Where's Simone and Ethan? No drinks tonight?"

"No, they were going back to their cabin. Not feeling social I guess. It's like some people come here to get away from people or something." Allie said. She laughed as she slid an empty beer across the wood grain to Molly's awaiting hands.

"Hey, if you wanna go back to the cabin, or skinny dip in the lake, whatever, we can go anytime," Jonah said.

"I'm not skinny dipping at night."

"You scared."

"No, I've never been scared a day in my life," Allie said.

"That's why I love you. Fearless, always fearless." Jonah drew Allie's hand to his mouth and kissed it. Molly watched them in awe. Everything about them seemed effortless.

"You two are amazing. I bet you'll be 80 years old and still so damned cute." Molly said. She folded her arms and drew in a deep breath.

"You and Zack seem to be pretty damn cute yourselves," Allie said as she sipped.

"Yeah, if I don't blow it."

"Oh, the moving in thing, huh?"

"Be fearless, Molly. Like this lady here. Just do it." Jonah said. His smile was contagious. He had a buoyancy about him, a hopefulness. Molly remembered when they married a year earlier at the resort. She could see in his eyes that he was madly in love with Allie. He was a romantic, an optimist about everything.

"I've never been fearless," Molly said.

"You can always start," Allie said.

As the night wore on, guests and locals filtered out of the lounge. The roar of laughter and music turned to the level of a lullaby.

"Hey, Mol. I'm gonna cut out for the night. I'll see you tomorrow. We got a band coming for the weekend, so I'll be in early. Oh, and a shipment coming, too." Carl said as he hung up his apron. "Unless you want me to stick around to clean up after these stragglers?"

"Nah, Carl. I got it. You go home." Molly said as she slid wine glasses on the shelf behind the bar.

"Molly, can I grab a flashlight to take down the trail?" Jonah asked. She nodded yes. He disappeared into the lodge. Allie took the last drink from her beer and stood.

"Hey, Allie, you guys be careful. There've been a few coyote sightings lately. Plus, you're wearing all black. Jonah will lose you in the dark." Allie laughed.

"I can find my own way." Allie pushed in the barstool. "Thanks for everything this week, Molly. We really needed this getaway. Well, I did at least."

"You guys coming back here has been the highlight of my summer. I hope you plan to make it an annual trip, even if you guys have kids soon." Molly noticed Allie's face drop. Her broad smile faded. "What? Is it something I said?" Molly ducked under the side of the bar and stood in front of Allie.

"No. Not really."

"You guys are trying, right? I thought I heard Jonah say that at dinner the other night."

"Well, Jonah wants to try right now. I'm not ready."

"Oh, I didn't realize. I thought you wanted kids right away, too."

"I do. God knows I do. But, Molly, I'm not sure it's gonna be easy for me." Allie glanced around her shoulder to be sure Jonah hadn't walked back in.

"Why? I mean, if you want to tell me. If not, I understand. Is there a fertility issue? My God, Allie, that's so common anymore."

"No, I know I can get pregnant. I just, I had a miscarriage a few months ago."

"Jesus. I'm sorry. And he wants to try again so soon?"

"He doesn't know, Molly. Please don't say anything to Zack or anyone. I didn't tell him. He was away for work when it happened. I meant to tell him. I did, I swear. But the words…" Allie wiped away a tear and swayed a little. Molly reached out and steadied her.

"It's okay, Allie. It's okay." Allie nodded and drew in a deep breath. "I won't say a word. I promise."

"It's just I don't want Jonah to see me as a failure. I don't want him to look at me like I look at myself now. Does that make sense? I know I have to tell him. But, I don't want to see the look in his eyes when he feels the loss of something we never had."

"But, you can't bear it alone, Allie. He could help you through it." Molly said. Allie shook her head.

"I'll help myself through it." She said. Jonah came through the door from the main lodge with a flashlight in hand.

"There you are, Jonah," Molly said. She squeezed Allie's shoulder as Allie wiped one more tear. Molly's heart sank as she watched them walk into the darkness. She marveled at Allie as she lost sight of them. Molly had considered Allie to be a real-life wonder woman. She was steadfast, wise, unstoppable. Molly couldn't believe she had been carrying around the pain, the loss, all alone. Molly wanted to chase her down the trail and beg her to let Jonah in, let him ease some of that burden. But, it wasn't her place. She thought of Zack and how she couldn't ever keep something like that from him. Molly knew nothing could kill a marriage or relationship quicker than secrets, even secrets kept with the intent of saving someone else from pain.

Just as she placed Allie's empty bottle in the recycling bin under the bar sink, Molly saw the man from earlier in the week. He was staring at her again.

"Hey, you over there. Can I help you." She yelled out. She glanced around and realized he was the only one left in the lounge. "It's kinda late. I know we're still open, but, as you can see, the place is closing down shortly." The man gave her a half smile and sipped from a bottle.

"You kicking me out, kid?" He said. "What about last call?"

Molly raised her eyebrows. "Okay, I guess it's last call." She felt uneasy and regretted sending Carl home early. Molly glanced around to spot her cell just in case she needed to call someone, anyone. The man strolled over and leaned his elbow on the bar. He swigged the last of his beer and slid the bottle to Molly.

"I'll take one more, kid." Molly opened another and walked it to him.

"Kid? I'm kinda old for that. But, that's neither here nor there. Who are you anyway? You look familiar, but I don't think I know you. You a friend of Carl's?"

He took a long drink, finishing nearly half the bottle. Molly's eyes widened.

"Nope. Just an old guy in town, driving down memory lane, I guess."

"Oh, did you used to come here when my parents ran the place?" Molly folded her arms. Her uneasiness started to grow.

"I used to come here, off and on. I came here this time to remember."

"Most people come here to forget." Molly quipped.

"I came here to remember your mother."

"Wha...wha...You knew my mom? I didn't get your name? Who are you?"

"Martin O'Neil. Marty to your mom."

"And my dad? If you knew my mom, you knew my dad. They were kinda a package deal running this place until she passed." Molly unfolded her arms. She noticed the roadmap of wrinkles across his weathered face softened. Marty took another deep gulp of his beer.

"Careful there, Mr. O'Neil. You don't seem to have a designated driver, and I know you aren't a guest here at the lodge."

"Guest. No, I'm no guest. Your dad woulda kicked my ass just for walking into this place. He'd never a let me rent a cabin. That's for sure." He snickered.

"Why's that? My dad wasn't the fighting kind." Molly felt dizzied and yet annoyed by his coyness. She put her hands on her hip. "Listen, what's your deal? Why are you here?"

"I told you. I came here to remember her. Rosemary Bordeaux." He finished his drink. Molly swallowed a lump in her throat. "I loved your mother."

She stepped back and folded her arms once again. Molly could feel her cheeks getting warm. "Well, most people who knew her, loved her. She was a great woman. Had a lot of friends in this town." Molly's heart beat faster, and she felt short of breath.

"I used to do deliveries here, years ago, when you were just a kid. Elementary age then a bit older? I'm not sure. Your mom and I, we used to talk a lot. A lot. I started looking for more excuses to stick around, deliver in the winter, anything." He rubbed his forehead and closed his eyes. "Kid, truth be told, I fell in love with her. God, I loved her."

"Well, she loved my dad. Then, she died. So, I guess that's the end of this story." Molly walked to the door and opened it. "Now, Mr. O'Neil, we're closed." Marty spun around on his barstool. He didn't stand up. Molly drew in another breath. "Listen. It's time to go, sir. I'm sorry if you have these old, pent-up feelings for my mom. But, she's been gone for well over 20 years. Her death devastated my dad. It plunged him into depression and alcoholism. He couldn't function after she died. It ruined my family. I'd rather not have a stranger come into my lounge and try to hijack our loss. My loss." He rubbed his chin and placed his skinny, age-spotted hands on his knees.

"Listen, Kid."

"Stop calling me kid. You aren't my parent. My parents are dead. Please leave."

"She was the love of my life. Her smile, her curves, her giggle. I can still hear her. I can—"

"Stop! I don't need to hear this. Whatever you felt for her had to be one-sided. Now listen. I'm done asking you. Just get out." Molly said. Her words didn't feel like they came from her mouth. She flinched and couldn't look him in the eye. Her gut seized, and her hands shook. A wave of anger she hadn't felt in a long time was bubbling.

"Kid, it wasn't one-sided. She loved me, too. We planned to run off together. Everything was set. We only had to wait a few more months, and then she had her accident. I had a place in Asheville, North Carolina. We had everything ready to start over down there." Marty closed his eyes again. Molly could see he was crying. She felt dizzy again. Her ears started to ring. Molly held her forehead.

"Is this a sick joke? My mom loved my dad. She wasn't all prepared to run off with anyone. I think I would've noticed that." Her voice cracked. "She wouldn't have left me or my dad willingly. Ever." Molly let go of the door and backed up towards the wall.

"Kid, I'm not here to upset you. I'm sorry. I just, I just drink and miss her. She was the love of my life. I miss what we could've had if she hadn't died in that car wreck in town. We were so close to starting a life together."

"What? Why are you saying these things? She wouldn't have left him or me. We lost everything when she died. My dad lost everything. He drank his life away after she died. He never got over losing her that way."

"Your dad did love her. Can't deny that. But he didn't drink his life away because she died."

"Yes, he did. You don't know anything about us. I don't care what you say you had with my mom."

Marty stood up. He towered over the bar and everything else in the lounge. Molly raised her eyes to his as he took a few steps forward. She fought back tears. Her head was spinning. She held onto the wall as he got closer.

"I'm sorry. I am. But your dad, Mason, drank his nights away because he found out about us months before she died. She told him she was leaving, and he lost it. Her death just kept everyone else from knowing she was leaving, from knowing about us at all." Marty reached out and touched her shoulder. Molly cringed and looked past him. "I never set out to tell you all this, kid. But, stepping back in here, seeing this place, it just brought it all back for me. I'll leave now. I'm sorry to have upset you." He squeezed her shoulder.

Molly slid out under his arm. She walked toward the bar. Her eyes scanned every inch of the lounge. She felt like she was sinking. Once she heard the door close, Molly darted over and locked it behind the man who had just sent her world into a tailspin.

Molly walked to the bar and slid onto a stool as his words still echoed in her head. It was like quicksand was pulling her down, meshing her to the bar and stool. Everything was in slow motion. She rested her elbows on the shiny, wood bar her father built so many years ago. She let her head fall into her hands as tears exploded from her eyes. "No, no," she said to herself as she shook her head and wiped her face on a bar napkin. "He's full of shit." She peered into the mirror behind the bar.

Molly squinted. She had her mother's chin, eyes, and nose. Molly thought back to her last memories of her mother. She remembered getting on the school bus and watching her walk up the lane, her mother's long dark hair swaying back and forth across the small of her back as she disappeared behind the pines that lined the driveway.

Molly closed her eyes to think back further. She pictured herself running through the lodge, around the stone fireplace that split the place in two. Then, the lounge. She remembered the faint sounds of her father crying, rambling, in the lounge late at night, long after the guests left. Molly had always associated those sounds with him mourning her mother. But, as Molly sat in that same lounge almost 30 years later, she realized she also heard her mother's footsteps, her heels, clicking across the pine lodge floors. Her mother wasn't dead in those days, that summer. Rosemary was leaving at night, in heels. Molly looked up at the mirror again. "Why would she be leaving in heels at night while dad sat in the lounge crying? No, those couldn't be the same nights or the same summer." Molly drew in a deep breath and let her herself sink further onto the stool. Those were the same nights. How had she never realized it before?

Molly strained to remember more. She could hear shouts, arguing, as she sat in bed reading. She remembered sliding down further and pulling the sheet over her head. Words weren't clear. Intentions weren't either. But, as she sat in the lounge, memories of that summer came floating to the surface. Her mother died in the fall, just after school started. Molly remembered red luggage bought when they were school shopping. It was luggage for her mother. Maybe Marty was telling the truth. If he was, had her childhood been a lie? She always associated Mason's drinking problem with her mother's death. It technically wasn't anyone's fault, at least that's what she told herself the last year. He descended into alcoholism because of circumstances beyond his control. They loved each other, deeply, and faithfully. If her mother hadn't died, they would've been a blissful, stable, happy family. Her parents' love meant real, lasting love was possible. But, it wasn't bliss and apparently, it wasn't faithful. Her mother planned to leave them, planned to leave her. Molly thought of the past year raising Emerson alone, sending her back and forth to Nashville. How could her mother have intended to leave her behind? Why hadn't her father told her any of this? He sat alone night after night, drinking, crying, mourning the love of his life. Only he wasn't mourning the loss of her to an unfortunate car accident, but to another man, then both.

Molly's red and confused eyes scanned the bar in front of her. The bottles were full of brown and clear comfort. She hadn't drunk anything other than a glass of wine here and there in over a year. She got up from the stool and ducked under the bar. Molly took a glass from underneath. She grabbed a bottle of bourbon. She poured the glass half full. Molly's breath quickened. Her temples pounded. Some bourbon splashed on the bar as she pulled the bottle back upright. Molly brought the glass to her lips. She tilted her head back and let the bourbon fill her mouth. Molly swallowed quickly, and the burn cascaded to her gut. She coughed. She drew the glass to her lips once more. Bourbon would absorb the confusion. Bourbon would help her forget everything Marty had said, and everything she had remembered. She could let bourbon erase the last hour and any revelations she didn't want to accept. Bourbon would make her childhood what she knew it to be yesterday. She filled her mouth again. She looked in the mirror and saw her mother's chin, eyes, and nose again. For the first time in her life, she didn't want to see her mother in her face. As she swigged more bourbon, she started to see her dad. How many nights did he spend alone, devasted that he couldn't hold on to the thing he needed and treasured most in the world—her mother and the life they had together? He already lost her before she had that accident. Now, decades later, Molly felt as if she had lost her mother all over again.

Molly remembered seeing her dad in that mirror last year when she hit rock bottom. She spit a mouthful of bourbon back into the glass. The bourbon wouldn't wash it all away. Molly knew she'd regret it in the morning. She squinted into the mirror. She didn't see her mother or father. Molly suddenly felt as if she didn't know who they were at all, or for that matter, who she was. Molly slammed the glass in the sink and put the bottle on the shelf. *Enough*, she told herself. *No more. This won't fix a damn thing.* Molly told herself.

She shuffled over the spot where her father had died and past the jukebox, where her mother's lover stood earlier. She turned out the light and went past the stone fireplace, the giant moose antlers, and down the hall. Molly retreated to the bedroom that had been her parents', a bedroom filled with love and promise, or so she had thought. She wasn't sure what to make of the truth that barreled into her consciousness that night. Drowning it with bourbon wouldn't work. It never did, Molly thought as she pulled her shirt off and crawled into bed. She pulled back the quilt. Molly crawled underneath and pulled it over her head. The fight with Zack days earlier lingered in her mind as the taste of bourbon lingered in her mouth. Both made her feel as if the week had been a giant failure. As she drifted off, Molly remembered her birthday on the roof. She had shouted her wish to the world, her wish for everything to stay the same. Suddenly, nothing was the same as that day, and she knew it might never be again.

Chapter 4

The Storm

Molly

The wind whipped through a small crevice in the wood around the bedroom window. As it swirled around the tiny log cabins in the clearing and the main lodge, it sounded like a siren. Most people feared lightning, thunder, and the tremendous force of hail. However, the wind was where the real power lies in a New England summer storm. It was unseen, unpredictable, and could be unrelenting. Some summer storms in Maine could bring a sigh of relief and leave behind drenched herbs, flowers, and trees that would glisten as sunlight returned within minutes. Others, if the wind came first, would leave destruction and trauma in their wake. Some summer storms and winds could permanently change the landscape.

Molly woke to a churning in her gut and a headache. She barely drank any, but after a year of nearly nothing, it sure didn't feel like just a little. Her phone vibrated on the nightstand. Before she reached for it, she noticed the curtain waving. Even though she and Zack had resealed the logs and updated windows, the wind could blow in when it was strong enough.

"Hello?" she said as she swiped answer.

"Why do you sound like shit?" Zack said. "You getting sick?"

"Long story, honey. What's up?"

"I was gonna let you know I'm taking Hannah to lunch in town then we'll be out to visit. Okay?"

"Yeah, okay. I'll get by without you." Molly said.

"Hey, don't forget we're supposed to get a crazy storm passing through today."

"Oh, yeah. I guess that's why the wind is whipping around out there. Pretty gusty from what I see from the bedroom."

"Yeah, just be on the lookout. I'll be out later."

Molly hung up and jumped out of bed. A rush of blood raced through her temples. They began to pound like tiny sledgehammers from the inside out. Molly drew in a deep breath and settled her body and mind. She shuffled to the bathroom. Molly reached down and turned on the shower. Blood rushed to her head again. The pounding stopped her in her tracks. She wasn't sure if it was a headache from the swigs of bourbon, or the drop in pressure from the impending storm. She stepped in and let the hot water bounce off her body. Marty's words came flooding back. The truth was still there, and there was nothing she could do to forget it. Molly fought the urge to cry again. She washed as clean as possible. As she got ready, put on a forced smiling face, and entered the main part of the lodge, she heard the wind whip louder. Molly felt it was engulfing everything.

She opened the main lodge doors. A gust nearly knocked her off her feet. She turned her head and held her hair out of her face as she stepped out. Molly raced to the gazebo to take the hanging pots of petunias down before they became unwilling projectiles. Just as she lowered one to the floor inside the gazebo, a shadow cast itself over the floor. It was Allie.

"Hey, what are you doing here? I thought you guys were heading to town today. Do some souvenir shopping." Molly said. Allie's long frame nearly reached to the top of the gazebo doorway. She wore another black t-shirt and shorts. Her tanned legs stretched for miles, at least in Molly's eyes.

"I just wanted to check on you. I got an uneasy feeling about that old man last night. And, well, you seemed a little bogged down. You okay?" Allie said. She reached her long arms to one of the hanging pots and unhooked it. "Plus, you're too short to get these all down alone."

Molly let a short laugh escape. "Yeah, he was interesting. Had quite a story to share before I asked him to leave." She said as she stood up and moved two of the pots into the center of the gazebo. "It's gonna be one helluva storm later, so I gotta get these all down."

"What kind of story?" Allie crossed her arms.

"Well, just between you and me, he claims he had an affair with my mom."

"What?" Allie uncrossed her arms and put her hands on her hip. "Jesus, did you ever know any of that? Maybe he's just crazy or something?"

"I hate to say it, but after I kicked him out, I got to thinking about stuff. I think he was telling the truth."

"Wow. I'm sorry. That had to be a kick in the gut, huh?"

"Yeah, you could say that." Molly leaned back on the railing of the gazebo. "He said she was gonna leave me and my dad and her death was the only thing that stopped her. He said my dad started drinking heavily because he found out. I had always assumed it was because he lost her. But, now I guess, it was a combination of the two."

"Jesus. Why'd he tell you any of this? Seriously, what kind of asshole waltzes in to tell someone something like that about their dead mom decades later?"

"I don't know, Allie. I don't know. But it really shook me last night. Shook me enough I swigged some bourbon, luckily not too much, but more than I've had in over a year." Molly exhaled and crossed her arms.

"Well, don't beat yourself up about that. Sometimes, it's needed, deserved. I know I've had a bit too much lately to deal with some shit."

"Yeah, but I got to a point last year where I felt it was needed and deserved way too much. Moderation wasn't in my vocabulary." Molly leaned up and scooted another pot to the center. The wind started to whip harder. She noticed thick, gray clouds rolled overtop the entire skyline. "Anyway, it just makes me rethink everything I thought I knew about my mother. It also makes me want to apologize to Simone for being a prick about her confiding in us. She seemed like she really needed to get stuff out and I kinda just shut her down."

"Yeah, I didn't expect that from her. But hey, don't let some random news about your mom make you think differently of her. You know? She was still your mom, right? A mom you loved to remember."

"Well, according to this guy, Marty was his name, she was gonna leave me. So, she wasn't just having an affair behind my dad's back. She was gonna leave me behind."

"You have no way of knowing what she would've done. It's his word against a ghost, really."

"Yeah, I guess. But honestly, Allie, looking back, I think she was preparing to leave us."

Allie walked over and hugged Molly. "She was a woman, not just a mom. Don't let one mistake or one potential mistake change who you knew her to be." Allie drew back. "Trust me. People are much more complex than that. And everyone has secrets, makes mistakes, bad decisions, has regrets. Hell, all of us go to bed at one point or another praying certain truths or certain lies don't surface." Thunder rattled the gazebo.

"Jeez, we better get inside the lodge," Molly said. They both sprinted to the lodge porch. "That's one angry sky."

"Yeah," Allie said as she looked up. "You can almost feel the electricity in the air."

"It's not supposed to start until later, after dinner. But, it's sure building up to be a strong one." Molly said. "The longer they take to build up, the stronger the storm will be."

"You got that right, I'm afraid," Allie said. She crossed her arms and followed Molly inside.

As Allie prepared a breakfast plate, Molly thought more about the storm and Marty. He just appeared, lingered for a night, and exploded truths all over the lounge, like a tornado. He changed everything in his wake once he walked out the door. His intentions were irrelevant. The damage was done. The more Molly thought about it, the more her visions of her entire childhood were altered, tainted. She started to picture her mom darting out the back door of the kitchen, just off the corner where the large stainless-steel dishwasher roared three times a day. Her mom would slither out to sneak cigarettes. Molly always caught a whiff of the smell every time she came back in. Molly remembered a guy out there with her, laughing. The delivery guy who brought bread and canned goods each week. He smoked with her. Molly remembered how she'd climb onto the counter next to the racks of steaming dishes. She'd hear her mother sounding happy, giddy. *That had to be Marty*, Molly thought to herself. He made her laugh in a way Molly couldn't remember her laughing anywhere else at the lodge. Molly's heart sank. Marty roared into their lives years ago and upended everything. Now, decades later, he rolled back to Moose Pond Lodge to throw everything into a tailspin again. Molly glanced around the clean, sterile kitchen. She thought of the laughs and dances with Zack as they cleaned up each night. She thought of the stolen kisses as he snuck up behind her while she pushed those racks of steaming dishes down the line. She trusted him and trusted in what they had. But suddenly, there was a heaviness in the air of that kitchen, the lodge. There was a gray cloud over all that made sense the last year. Letting Zack move in wouldn't help her figure out what it all meant, who she was, who her parents really were. It would just cloud everything more.

As Molly cleaned up and completed daily duties around the lodge, she tried to conjure more images of her mother and that summer. She squinted as she tried to recall the sounds of the bands on weekends, the clicks of heels dancing, the sounds of glasses clinking with endless toasts about the best summers ever. Her mind would always wander back to the faint sounds of her father alone in the lounge. Then, the sounds of Molly fighting with him, yelling, slamming doors as a teenager surfaced. Her heart raced as she remembered calling him a sad, lonely drunk. Molly bowed her head and rested her hand on the top of a broom when the image of his face absorbing those words came to light. Why didn't he ever tell her about her mother? Did he intentionally sacrifice his image in Molly's mind to preserve her mother's? Molly exhaled. Regret weighed down on her shoulders.

She raised her head to the sound of the large wooden doors opening. Before she could turn around, she felt a thud against the back of her thighs. It was a full-speed embrace from Hannah. Molly let the broom fall as she turned to hug her back.

"Hey! How's my favorite five-year-old doing?" Molly said.

"I'm good. I miss Emerson. When's she coming home?" Hannah said as she gripped Molly tight. Her brown curls bounced as she ran around Molly's legs.

"Soon. About a week or so." Molly said. Zack pulled her arm and enveloped her. As Zack and his daughter embraced Molly, a pang radiated from her heart as she thought of the one thing missing—Emerson.

Molly melted into the leather couch across from the stone fireplace and told Zack about the conversation with Marty. Her eyes followed Hannah as she danced around the fireplace. Hannah never stopped moving. Molly had fallen in love with the sprite in the last year. Seeing her, feeling her hugs, and hearing her high-pitch giggle made Molly's heart melt as she remembered Emerson at that age.

"So, basically, I feel like I don't even know my mom now," Molly said. Zack squeezed her hand. He leaned over and kissed her shoulder.

"Well, I think I've got something to cheer you up even though I didn't know you needed cheering up," Zack said. Molly furled her forehead. Zack stood and pulled her to her feet. "Follow me to the truck." Hannah jumped up and down a dozen times in one spot.

"Is it time, Daddy?" She squealed as she clapped her hands. Her curls vibrated with each clap.

"What are you two up to?" Molly asked as Zack led her to the door. Hannah pushed on her butt behind her. Zack told her to wait on the porch as he sprinted across the parking lot to his truck. Molly held Hannah's hand as she continued to jump up and down. As the door to the truck creaked shut, Molly saw Zack emerge with a ball of fur in his arms. Sharp yips came from the furry creature. Molly gasped.

"What is that? What have you done, Zack Preston?" Her hair blew in front of her eyes.

"It's a puppy!" Hannah yelled. She let go of Molly's hand and ran to the steps to pet it. Zack held it down for a closer look.

"He's a yellow lab. He's a spitfire but look at those eyes. He's a smart one. I can tell." Zack held him up and rubbed noses with him. He handed him to Molly. The dog squirmed and licked her face as Molly drew him near.

"What's his name?" Molly giggled as the wet nose and tongue swarmed her face.

"Don't know yet. I figured we could decide together. Maybe wait till Em gets home? Take a family vote?"

"I vote banana! No, no I vote butter. It has to be something yellow, right?" Hannah said. She squealed and reached for the wagging tail. Molly leaned down to get closer to Hannah.

"Zack, you don't have to wait for Em. You and Hannah should decide. He's your dog." Zack leaned down and clipped a leash to a blue collar with white bones on it. The puppy bounced and bucked like a wild animal.

"Hang on there, buddy. I'll get you on the grass." Zack said as he led the dog off the porch. Hannah and Molly followed.

"I love him. I love him. I love him." Hannah said as she scrambled for his tail. The puppy leaped for her nose.

"He's our dog, Mol. I got him for the four of us. I had already arranged to get him when I brought up you know." He mouthed 'moving in' while raising his eyebrows at Hannah. "He is supposed to be our family dog. And think about it, Molly. What summer lodge doesn't have a great dog?" He winked at her. Molly's smile while playing with the rambunctious puppy slid away.

"Zack, we talked about that. You know I love what we've got going on here. I need time. And after hearing all this stuff about my mom, well, I feel like I'm totally out of sorts. I don't know what to make of all of it right now. I gotta process a lot." She crossed her arms and stepped back onto the step.

Zack drew in a deep breath. He gave Hannah the leash. "Here, sweetie. Take him in the gazebo and don't let him go. Okay?" Hannah nodded as she skipped with the dog in tow. Zack walked closer to Molly. "Dammit. It's always gonna be something, huh?"

"What's that supposed to mean?"

"The first time I kissed you last summer you drew back. You pushed me away. You were in the middle of a divorce then. Then, after Hannah's accident and I made the biggest mistake ever by thinking I should get back with her mom, I got why you wanted to take things slow when I came back wanting to try this again. And, you also wanted to take things slow because of the drinking. You needed to get a handle on that. I understood. I held back, gave you room, just let things be kinda casual—your word for this, not mine." Zack glanced behind him to check on Hannah and the dog. "You got a handle on all that, and I've been cool with you doing your whole 'all things in moderation' mantra."

Molly noticed Zack's blue eyes got a little darker. They always did when he was upset, or so it seemed.

"What's wrong with that? Meditating, focusing on moderation in all areas of my life has helped get through this year. It's why I feel better than I've ever felt. I'm a better mom because of it. How dare you say it like it's a bad thing." Molly said as she stepped up one more step on the porch, increasing the space between them. She looked up at the sky and noticed deeper gray and black in the clouds above.

"Nothing's wrong with it, Molly, but I'm not a habit to 'moderate.' I want to believe being with me might've helped you get through this year, too, not just scooting on that damn roof and meditating and avoiding bourbon. Damn, girl. I just want to love you. I just want you to come to your damn senses and see me as more than the help around here or something casual. You can't hold me at arm's length forever. And, you sure as hell can't use whatever this guy said your mom did as another reason to hold back."

"I need to know what she did, why she did it. You don't understand, Zack. This changes---"

"Nothing!" Zack tossed his arms in the air. Molly was startled by how loud he suddenly got. "Jesus. That has nothing to do with me and you. Nothing at all. You're not your mom. Hell, you're not your dad either. We aren't your parents. Don't you see that?" Zack shook his head. "Hannah, come over here and get your shoes from the porch, honey." The girl bobbed past the gazebo and bounced up the steps. She steadied herself against Molly's leg as she slid her sandals on and held the leash.

"I know that. I need time. It's a lot to take in. I know I'm not her or him and we aren't them. But, they're part of me so, yeah, it does affect me even if you don't want it to. And frankly, Zack, bringing a dog here to woo me into letting you move in is a pretty low blow."

"If you consider me wanting to be a family with you and our kids a 'low blow' then we need to rethink this whole thing." Zack reached for Hannah's hand. "Molly, I know I only have half your heart right now. I know that's all you want to give. But I'm beginning to think it'll never be more. I've fooled myself into thinking half of you was better than nothing. And honestly, since I broke your heart last summer, I kinda thought I only deserved half for a while. But, shit, sorry Hannah, I want more and, well, you don't." Zack said as he patted the girl's head. "I've been carrying a ring in that truck for the last two months. I'm done with this moderation bullshit. I'm done with only having half your heart. We either dive into this thing now or never. Seriously, Mol. Either we take this to the next level or I guess I'm out. I need more, and you aren't ready, or willing, to give it." Zack turned and walked toward the truck. Molly's gut seized.

"Zack, wait," Molly said. Hannah turned her tiny head and waved at Molly as Zack led her and the dog across the parking lot. He slid the puppy into the back seat and helped Hannah into her booster seat. Molly was unable to breathe. A ring was in that truck. Zack and Hannah were in that truck. She thought of running across the parking lot to stand in front of him, stop him from leaving, even though the last thing she wanted was a ring. But, her legs were planted firmly on the steps as the wind whistled past. She exhaled as he started the truck. As he lurched forward, he paused and leaned out the window.

"I'm serious, Molly. Quit trying to sift through or figure out the past, trying to figure out what it means for you or us. Look ahead for once. Either you see us as a family, or you don't. And, I'm guessing by the sounds of it, you don't." He leaned back in and drove to the end of the driveway. Molly gasped as she watched the truck disappear behind the pines as he made it to the main road that would take him back to town, to his house. A crack of lightening broke her teary trance. She jumped and felt a thud in her chest. The hair on her arms stood straight up. The electricity in the air made her take another step up toward the porch. Molly finally had everything she wanted and all she wanted was for it all to remain the same. As she watched a storm move closer, she realized by wanting it all to stay the same she might lose everything. Molly heard another slow, echoing crack in the woods and knew a tree was falling somewhere. It was taking others down with it. She turned and walked to the large wooden doors of the main lodge. She had crossed through those giant doors thousands of times during her life. When she crossed that threshold a little more than a year earlier, Molly had no idea what she'd find, and she certainly didn't plan to stay. She took a lodge full of her father's demons and made it a lively, happy place again. She turned the very place she ran *from* at 18 into a place she proudly ran *to* at the end of each day. She had made it hers and hers alone, her true home. But, Molly had always pictured her mother loving it there, too. The revelation that her mother was ready to abandon Moose Pond Lodge, her father, and her, was like a giant tree crashing through her world. Molly felt like she was letting it take out everything else around her, too.

Another crack of thunder rattled the porch. Molly cringed and entered the lodge just as the sky unleashed a driving rain. She hurriedly sent a mass text to all her guests telling them to remain indoors or seek shelter. Molly ran to the dining room and pulled the windows shut just as lightning flashed from beyond the pines. A split second later, thunder rumbled from the floor and through her body. She heard the distinct crack of another tree collapsing in the woods. As she went to the window closest to the main lodge door, she saw Zack's truck fly back into the driveway. Her heart stopped. It came to a halt right next to the steps, feet from the gazebo and grass. Molly ran to the door and swung it open. The wind and rain were deafening. Zack jumped from the driver's side and raced around to the passenger side. He grabbed Hannah from her seat and tossed her to the third step.

"Take her in! It's bad down the road." He yelled as he slammed the door shut. Zack reached into the back seat and pulled out the shaking puppy. Molly covered Hannah's head and rushed her under the porch roof. Mere seconds of exposure soaked the child. Zack jumped the steps by twos and joined them as they crossed into the sanctuary of the main lodge doors.

"My God, Zack," Molly said as she slid Hannah down.

"A huge tree is blocking the road. Fell right in front of me. Just as I turned around to get back here, another fell. It was like a foot from the bed of the truck."

"You okay, honey?" Molly said to Hannah as she pulled her wet hair from her face.

"Yeah. I'm cold now, though." Hannah said in her little voice.

"I'll take her to the bathroom. She needs dry clothes on. I'll dig out something from Emerson's room." Molly scooped up Hannah and took her down the hall. Thunder violently shook the lodge again. Molly paused to hear if another tree fell. Her phone started to vibrate. As she put Hannah down on the floor, she saw a flurry of texts. Allie and Simone were both telling her thunder was rattling cabins and trees falling were scaring them.

"If you feel like you can make it to the lodge safely, then please try. But be careful. This storm is horrible." Molly texted to them both. *"Are your husbands there with you guys?"* Both Allie and Simone responded 'yes.' Molly let out a deep sigh. As rattled as she was by the thunder, trees falling, and Zack racing back to the lodge, she could

only imagine how scared her guests were as they hunkered down in tiny cabins.

As she and Hannah entered the main lodge, other guests had gathered around the stone fireplace. Zack was calming frayed nerves, which in turn, calmed Molly's. Zack picked up Hannah and kissed her forehead.

"Where's the dog?" Molly asked. Zack nodded to the kitchen door.

"He's scared of the thunder. Shaking like a leaf. He ran in there and hid under the sink. That's when everyone started coming in." Zack leaned over and kissed Molly's forehead. She relaxed her shoulders for the first time all day.

"I'm so glad you're here."

"Me, too. Not happy about the way we ended up getting back here. But, I'm glad you're not here alone."

"Me, too. Zack, I'm sorry about earlier. I am." Molly reached for his hand. The moment he got in his truck and pulled away with Hannah and the dog seemed like hours ago.

"Whatever. You just want to see that ring in my truck." He said. She laughed. He kissed her forehead again. "Seriously, after this storm, we need to figure this out. I meant what I said, Molly. I'm done with half your heart, half your time. It's all or nothing."

Even though she essentially ran the place alone and had worked to make it her own, she realized just how much Zack did for her and her home. Relying on him wasn't just because he was a strong man who could clear the path or fix the gazebo steps. He wasn't just the muscle behind what she couldn't lift, move, or break down. Zack also wasn't just the man who shared her bed a few nights a week and made her feel an intimacy she got lost in on those nights. He was so much more than that. His presence, his essence, his voice, the nudges of her side, and those subtle kisses on her forehead were more. Molly suddenly felt foolish for the things she said minutes earlier. In front of her was a man who wanted to be a family with her and Emerson. In more than ten years of marriage to Kenny the Philanderer, Emerson's father, she never felt he wanted their little family. He certainly wouldn't have fought for it. Molly realized she had fought Zack every step of the way for months, nearly a year. All her reasons for holding back, wanting a distance between them, seemed to fall to the wayside. As she stood next to Zack waiting and praying the next falling tree of the thick Maine woods wouldn't crash through her lodge, she realized he already was her family. Molly wondered if anyone else had ever felt so ridiculous, oblivious, and lucky all at the same time. Molly looked at him drying Hannah's hair with a towel, making sure everyone in the lodge was safe. She realized she let him back in a year ago, but she hadn't done much to deserve him and all he did for her. She admitted to herself that part of holding back was a punishment for leaving her last summer. She smiled thinking he wanted her anyway. She might've acted like a fool pushing away the best man she'd ever known, but there he was, still trying to get into her heart and protect her. She vowed to be the woman he deserved once the calm came after the storm, that is if he'd still give her the chance.

A blinding flash followed immediately by an echoing boom filled every space around the huddled bunch. Hannah screamed as Molly's heart made a thud against her chest wall. She grabbed her chest as if her heart was going to fly right out onto the floor. Her ears rang, and she saw spots. Zack pulled her close into this chest. A loud crack and crash replaced the ringing. Molly knew in that instant lightening had hit the lodge or a structure on the property. She shuddered and clutched Zack's side. Her gut seized as she thought of the remaining guests still out there somewhere. Molly knew whatever was left behind after this storm wasn't going to be pretty. Someone was going to get hurt and the damage might be unbearable for them all.

Chapter 5

The Storm

Simone

Simone's hands shook as she picked up her brush. She noticed her face was paler than usual when she glanced up at her reflection.

"You okay, honey?" Ethan asked from the other side of the bathroom door. Simone ran the brush through her red hair.

"Yes. I'm fine. Just a little nervous, you know? I'll be out in a minute." She shouted out to him.

"I know. I think we'll be fine riding it out here. I'll check the radar map on my phone though. If there's a lull, maybe we could take off for the main lodge."

"That's exactly what Molly just texted to me." She felt a slight ripple of relief that both Molly and Ethan had thought a safe sprint to the lodge was possible. Her heart was racing. Storms always caused a well of anxiety to bubble to the surface. But, the memory of one storm came roaring back every time she heard the cracks of thunder and saw flashes of lightning. Simone closed her eyes and wished she was at her beach house, or in the city. When it came to storms, she preferred to be safe at the beach house, overlooking the sea with a blanket of gray clouds rolling over the top. Even when the wind would pick up, and the surf would crash ashore, she could stand behind the French doors of the balcony terrace and watch the beauty of nature's wrath unfold. Regardless of how intense any storm outside of those doors got, she felt safe, removed, and untouchable. But, this storm wasn't offshore. It wasn't a rolling blanket of fluffy gray with the occasional flash of white lightning to illuminate the sea for miles. It was close and electric, and it reached through the tiny log cabin. Her jaw ached from clenching her teeth.

Simone let her mind drift to that fearful trip as a kid, her only other time venturing into the woods or mountains with her father, Andrew Forrester. Everyone called him Ash. He, like his father and his father's father, was a hunter and fisherman whenever the world of high finance and real estate could spare him for a week or two each year. When he couldn't get away for extended trips, he would take a day trip into the woods of upstate New York or the Berkshires. Despite her full schedule of dance, art classes, language lessons, piano, and regular school classes, Ash insisted Simone join him one day and overnight. She was twelve. Simone was more interested in boys, make-up, and coercing her mother into paying for headshots. She begrudgingly packed an overnight bag and slid into her father's new Jeep, which he only bought for his pretend-safari getaways less than a few hours from Manhattan and Greenwich. Simone remembered thinking he looked like a boy playing dress-up as he donned a safari hat and khakis. Simone smiled at the image of her father like that and wondered if that's how she looked to everyone when she arrived at Moose Pond Lodge.

On that day trip, they spent the day stopping for ice cream, settling in at a bed and breakfast tucked away in the rolling hills of the Berkshires, and then they set out for a hike. All she had was her school gym shoes and a windbreaker to fend off the chill that still lingered in the air. It was the kind of April where spring was slow to take hold. She remembered letting her eyes follow the slivers of sunlight along the trail as her father rattled off details of a moose hunt in Maine, an elk hunt in Colorado, and fishing in South Dakota. He was in the midst of advising her to ditch the makeup and ballet and always find a way to enjoy nature when the slivers of sunlight disappeared. Ash slowed down and held his hand up. "That doesn't look good," she remembered him saying in a low voice. Before Simone could reach him or ask what he saw, a loud crack reverberated from the sky to the ground under her feet. The dirt shook, the white flash of lightning blinded her, and she screamed. Ash reached back for her, but she turned and ran down the trail as fast as she had ever attempted to run in her life. The sound of a tree accepting defeat and slowly losing its life played in slow motion through the ringing in her ears. She ran off the trail and straight towards the most enormous tree she could see. Simone ducked behind it and cowered against its trunk. She hated the feel of the bark scraping her windbreaker as she rocked back and forth with her knees tucked to her chin. Simone remembered hearing her father yell her name, then scream it with a fevered intensity, but she was too terrified to answer. She wanted the world to stop and the sun to break through again. Simone never knew how long she was hiding before Ash found her. Once he did, he screamed at her about running away and hiding. He tried to explain that cowering under a tree instead of following him back to the clearing was the worst thing she could've done. But, his words bounced off her. All Simone remembered thinking was that she'd never go into the woods again. She'd stay surrounded by concrete or behind the glass doors of the family beach house. She would never expose herself to the unknown again, run the risk of being trapped, or electrified by nature. That bolt of lightning had paralyzed something in her. It had created a fear she never felt before and never wanted to feel again. As she stood in the bathroom of her cabin at Moose Pond

Lodge, she felt that same fear resurface. Only this time, she couldn't cower anywhere until it passed.

Simone shook her head and reached down for her jasmine perfume. *You're not in the woods of the Berkshires,* she told herself. She smelled the nozzle of the perfume bottle and closed her eyes. She heard the pounding of the rain pick up. The pinging started to wear on Simone's nerves as much as the thunder. She glanced at her phone. Simone suddenly regretted erasing all of Angel's texts. She wanted to reread his words, reimagine the feeling of his arms around her that afternoon. Simone licked the bottom of her lip as she looked back into the mirror. She let the memory of Angel's lips on hers take her away from the cabin and the storm for a moment. Everything fell silent for a second before a crack pierced the atmosphere again. Simone gasped and put down the bottle of jasmine. She reached for the door handle and opened it to find Ethan still standing right on the other side.

"Come here. I know you're petrified." He said with open arms. Simone walked into him and rested her head on his shoulder. He patted her back. "I don't think we should try to get to the main lodge. We're right in the middle of the worst of it, according to the weather on my phone." Simone nodded.

"Yeah, that's what I was afraid of. Guess we have to ride it out here. I wish we'd have just gone to the beach house." She said as she pulled back from him. He rubbed her shoulders.

"Hey now. We've had a nice week here. Got you into those woods to hike and even swim in the pond. The nights have been exceptionally great." He said with a smirk. She smiled back at him.

"Yeah, they have. I just hate that we're trapped here. You know what I think about storms like this."

"We'll be fine in here. I promise."

"You can't promise that."

"Hey, haven't I always kept you safe?" Ethan asked.

"Yeah."

"Protected? Sheltered from anything bad? Huh? Haven't I?"

Simone swallowed a lump in her throat. She stepped back and sat in the chair next to the fireplace. The word sheltered lingered in the air.

"I don't need to be sheltered, you know? I can take care of myself. Well, if I had to."

Ethan sat on the edge of the bed. "I didn't mean it in a bad way. But, come on, let's face it. You've had a pretty sheltered life. I mean, really, literally in fact. This is only the second time ever that you've set foot in the woods. You've been protected from anything bad in the world first by your dad, your family, then by me."

"The number of times one goes into the woods isn't an indicator of a sheltered life, Ethan. Just because I can't hunt, fish, or skin a deer doesn't mean I'm not a strong or independent woman." Simone crossed her arms.

"I didn't say that. Obviously, no one would ever expect you to hunt for your dinner, honey." He laughed. "But, when we got together, you and your family needed me to protect you, protect your reputation. Or rather, help you rebuild what reputation they kept intact for you."

Simone cringed and tilted her head. She started to wring her hands.

"Let's face it, my dear, without my help, God knows where you'd be right now." Ethan rested back on his elbows on the bed. "Sounds like it's slowing down a bit. Maybe we can take off in a few minutes," he said as he looked up.

"Where'd I be right now? Listen, I think I'd be doing pretty fine if you must know. It's not like I was some kind of sewer rat you rescued. My God, I was Simone Sterns-Forrester. My family has more money and clout than yours if you really want to go there, my dear." She sat up tall and crossed her arms again. Simone could feel her fingers ache as she balled her fist tight.

"That might be true, but it wasn't about money. No amount of money would've erased those stories about you being on the streets for a year in New York. My God, everyone believed you turned into some kind of junkie down there, running around with Hispanics in alleys, stealing food from dumpsters. All of Greenwich was abuzz with rumors for that whole year. Your family couldn't go out without questions, theories, and hell, so many people shunned them in general. It wasn't until my family accepted you and I touted you all over on my arm that people stopped making up shit about that year." Ethan sat up. His voice rose to a level Simone hadn't heard in years. "It was only because of me that anyone in society believed you had a breakdown and that you were fine now. Jesus. Simone, I saved you from complete ruin. But sometimes, honestly, I wonder if you even appreciate anything I've done. You seem to let your mind wander elsewhere, not even noticing when I'm talking to you half the time. Maybe you really did have a breakdown or something down there, for all I know."

Simone shot out of the chair. She thrust her arms stiff at her sides. She dug her nails into her palms.

"Dammit, Ethan, I wasn't crazy! I didn't have a breakdown! I was in love. Love. You hear me? A kind of love you'd never understand. I loved him, and I didn't want to leave and return to fucking Greenwich ever! If I seem to wander off, it's because I'm thinking of that year and who I was then. Who I was with him. Who I wanted to be with him, and how I was desperately in love with him! I still am, Dammit!"

Simone gasped after the words escaped her lips. She had never yelled at Ethan like that. He exhaled and stood in front of her. A perplexed look crossed his face. Simone felt he was looking like a stranger on the street would stare and study her face. Simone took a step back and sunk into the chair again. She shook her head in disbelief over the words that she had spit out at Ethan. Anger, disappointment, and pure fury flashed from his eyes. His cheeks grew red. He huffed like a bull ready to charge. She clenched her aching hands into a tighter fist. She was queasy. Simone parted her lips as she searched for anything to say to rescind what she had already unleashed.

Before a word could find its way to her tongue, a flash of white made her recoil in the chair. She drew up her legs. Her heart hurt as the floor rumbled and the sound of a devastatingly close crack vibrated through the cabin. Before she could rise, Ethan looked straight up. The ceiling crumbled above them as if it was made of paper. All Simone could see was brown and gray bark and pine branches. She had no time to scream, jump out of the way, or push Ethan back. An entire tree had decimated the roof of the cabin they rented to get away from chaos, stress, and their boring, predictable life in Greenwich. It was all destroyed in an instant. The tree groaned as it settled from one end of the cabin to the other. The bathroom door creaked, and glass shattered on the other side. She could barely see the bed where they made love all week. Simone gasped as she tried to comprehend what had just happened. The wet needles shook as the tree settled further. Simone felt the rain wash over her face and hair. She slowly stood on the seat of the chair. Simone noticed red on her arms as she steadied herself to peer across what was left of the room. She saw Ethan's leg. Then she traced his outline to find his face. He was bloodied, scratched by branches. She heard him moan as she struggled to get enough air in her lungs to talk.

"Oh dear, God. Ethan? Are you okay?" Her voice trembled. She heard him moan again. He coughed. Simone squinted and saw blood oozing from his nose and mouth. She drew her hand to her heart. Her eyes raced to locate every part of his body under the giant pine. She could see a branch across his chest and a deep gash on his legs. Simone had never seen that much blood before. She scanned the wreckage to find a way off the chair and over to what remained of the front door. She'd have to climb over the tree trunk and Ethan's lower body. Simone froze. Before she stepped down off the chair, she studied his face, the blood, the bubble on the edge of his mouth, his eyes closed. She studied his deep breath and waited for another moan.

"Simone." He said in a whisper. "Get help." More blood appeared on his dirty lips. Simone took a step off the chair. Her legs froze again. The bark, needles, and rain all engulfed her senses. The smell of earth in what was their shelter was choking her. She was paralyzed just as she was when she hid behind the tree at 12. Then, her entire relationship with Ethan rolled through her mind. It unraveled in a flash all the way to the point seconds ago when she told him who had her heart. Angel. She saw him in front of her. Simone exhaled and realized a life with Angel was within reach. If Ethan's ended right there on the floor of Cabin 3 at Moose Pond Lodge, she could disappear into Angel's world once again. Only this time, she'd be an adult whose family couldn't rip her back to Greenwich in a flash. She'd be free to wipe out her accounts or give up her money altogether, and show up at that apartment. She could spend the rest of her days intertwined with him, wrapped in bliss. She could experience the freedom and love she daydreamed about every chance she got. Simone could be who and what she wanted in a clean instant. There'd be no messy divorce. No rumors. No shame and slander. There'd be no look of horror or disdain for her in his face again. There'd be no sheltering, and there'd be no more sense of owing him everything, including herself. She could stand there for a few minutes and get another chance at the life she wanted without her old one ending in a dirty, unseemly way. It would be an unfortunate and tragic accident. Society would drape her in sympathy and go on without missing a beat as she slowly slid off their radar. Yes, she thought, she'd have to play the dutiful widow for a few months before leaving Greenwich to 'start over' somewhere new. Her eyes widened at the possibility of a clean getaway from life in Greenwich, from Ethan, and everything being Mrs. Simone Sterns-Forrester

Beckwith carried with it. Her mind raced with thoughts of showing up at Angel's door. The passion, the love, the sense of finally being awake again. It filled her mind and body like a flood. Despite the rain running down her face, she grew warm, even hot. Her heart raced, and her temples pounded. Then, another moan from Ethan pierced the dead silent air and her daydream of another life. Simone inhaled and looked around again. *Dear God, what am I doing?* She said to herself.

"Oh my God, Ethan, hang on. Please hang on, darling. I'm getting help!" She screamed at him. Simone shook her head and realized for a brief second of her life, she was willing to let Ethan die rather than be honest with him or herself. She was on the verge of letting him slip away out of pure cowardice and convenience.

Simone climbed over the trunk of the tree and felt branches scrape her legs. One latched onto to her hair. She pulled and broke free so she could reach Ethan's face. She maneuvered her arm through a branch and cluster of needles so she could touch his forehead. "I'm going for help. Please hang on, darling. I love you." She said through tears. She felt him nod slightly. Simone climbed further and pushed through what was left of the door. She could squeeze it open enough to slither out. As she got onto the porch, she heard him moan again. Simone felt she could throw up over her hesitation, her complete selfishness. Simone ran into the clearing and screamed for help. A guttural yell echoed above her as she dropped to her knees. The mud sloshed around her jeans, and the rain drenched every ounce of skin she had showing. Simone knew at that moment if Ethan didn't make it, she wouldn't be able to live with herself. And if he did, she had no idea what kind of life she'd have or deserve to have.

Chapter 6

The Storm

Allie

Allie screeched and grabbed Jonah's arm as the sound of a tree crashing through a nearby cabin echoed.

"That was definitely close. Too close." Jonah said as he drew her head against his.

"That hit a cabin. I know it."

A shriek penetrated the thick, electric air. The screams for help were coming from the clearing. Allie rushed to the window and pulled back the linen curtain. She saw Simone drenched and on her knees in the middle of the clearing.

"God, Jonah. It's Simone screaming." Allie said as she dashed across the cabin for her shoes. Jonah rushed to the door behind her. They raced through the rain to reach her. Simone was shaking and crying. Allie pulled her to her feet. Allie's ears were ringing from the thunder. Simone pointed to her cabin. Allie and Jonah both took a step back as their eyes absorbed the extent of the damage.

"Ethan's still in there! He's hurt!" Simone yelled through the continuous cracks of thunder. Allie flinched. She ducked as the lightning lit up the sky around them.

"There's a first aid kit in our bathroom. I'll grab it and go in there. You two get under our porch where it's safe. Call for help." Jonah pulled Allie's arm as she grabbed Simone's. As they got under the safety of the small porch, Allie hugged the shaking and wet red-head.

"How bad is it?" Allie asked. She was afraid of the answer. Jonah darted past and ran into the bathroom. He threw open the door of the medicine cabinet. Allie heard a crash. The first aid kit had fallen to the floor. Allie went the doorway and could see Jonah squat to the floor to gather the contents. She gasped as she remembered her birth control pills were hidden inside. Before she could step closer, she saw Jonah pick up the pack. He shook his head and turned the case around. He held it close to his face. She could tell he was squinting. Allie's shoulders slumped when she saw the color drain from his profile. He looked at her from the floor of the bathroom as she walked closer to him. Before she could make it to Jonah, he threw the pack against the wall. Allie cringed. She reached for him as he gathered a bandage. His eyes met hers for a second. She gasped at the mix of rage and despair in his eyes. Jonah pushed past her and took a pillow from a pillowcase and gathered up the sheet.

"I can use this if he's bleeding a lot," Jonah said. Allie again reached for his arm again. He swatted her away. "Don't Allie. Don't." Jonah dashed onto the porch. "Simone, call for help." He shouted as he disappeared out of sight. Allie's gut sank. Her arms were suddenly heavy. Her legs filled with lead. She had never seen Jonah look like that, discombobulated, shook. He was the most steady, solid man she'd ever known. He always had an answer, a plan. He always knew their next move, her next step. There was a place, a pace, a time, a phrase, an emotion for everything. There was never a second of faltering or uncertainty. But, now there was. It was written all over his face. She moved her hand over her abdomen. She felt sick. Her entire world had just left that cabin and entered a storm she couldn't control.

Simone rushed in and asked for her phone to call for help. She broke Allie from her spell. Allie blinked and resolved herself to the fact that she'd have to wait to explain to Jonah. She'd have to pray he'd understand once she told him the truth. Allie tried to focus as Simone rattled off the address to Moose Pond Lodge to the dispatcher on the other end of the phone. Then, she called Molly in a panic and told her to direct the ambulance their way. Allie grabbed the quilt from the bed and draped it over Simone's shoulders. She noticed Simone was still shivering. Allie reached her arm around Simone's shoulder.

"He's gonna be okay. If anyone can help him, it's Jonah. He'll make sure he's okay until help arrives."

Simone began to cry again. Allie rubbed her shoulder more. Allie could no longer tell if Simone's face was wet from the storm or tears. She seemed to be gushing water from every pore. Allie felt helpless to comfort her.

"I can't just wait here. I need to see him. Oh God, I was going to lea...to leave him there. I was gonna leave him, Allie." Simone said. Her eyes looked blankly ahead.

"What do you mean, leave him?" Allie asked. She wanted to wipe Simone's face, but she knew it was no use. "We heard you scream. You were frantic to get help for him."

Simone bowed her head. Her wet red hair clung to her face and neck. "I wanted a way out." Her words spilled out quietly when she exhaled. Her shoulders sank as her arms melted to her side. Allie stepped back and stared at her. She had spent the week seeing Simone as a shrinking violet, as a fragile new creature. She pictured her as too clean for the woods, for Moose Pond Lodge. Too pure to be sullied by dirt, by life. Simone was a label, an object defined by the string of last names she attached to herself. But as she stood in front of her during a horrendous storm, with blood on her shirt and regret bearing down on her shoulders, Allie saw there was much more to Simone than she had perceived. Her purity, paleness, lightness, was suddenly dark and sad. Allie drew her hand up to Simone's chin. She lifted it and met her eyes.

"Hey there. I don't know exactly what's going on, but I'm sure this is all gonna work out. Everything's gonna be okay." Allie told her once again. This time, Allie wasn't quite sure it would, and not just for Simone and Ethan, but also for her and Jonah.

The whirl of sirens pierced through the downpour as did residual cracks of thunder. It broke the spell between the two women. Allie grabbed Simone's hand.

"Come on," Allie said as she dragged the pale, soaked lump of a former model. She felt Simone go partially limp. "Come on," Allie said again.

The two stepped off the porch of the cabin just as the rain slowed to a trickle. Allie could still feel the electricity in the air. The ambulance was backing into the clearing. The clearing seemed to open and absorb the giant vehicle. Allie was afraid it would get stuck. She led Simone through the soggy earth to what was left of the cabin. The debris was at their feet.

"Jonah? Is he okay?" She called through the fractured doorway. She saw the top of Jonah's head through the tree that had dissected the cabin. She heard Ethan moan as Jonah reassured him help had arrived.

"Back, please," a voice from behind said. Allie moved away and gently led Simone with her. The buzz of a chainsaw startled her. She squeezed Simone's hand. Simone gasped and held her free hand over her mouth. Branches were removed, and needles rustled and bounced on the ground below. Everything was wet and heavy. Allie noticed the smell. It wasn't the familiar and peaceful smell of a summer storm, the kind she relished filling her lungs with as a kid in Georgia. It was earthy but in a treacherous way. It reminded Allie that despite how much she tried to control her surroundings, trust in her instincts in the woods and water, under trees, she was at the mercy of forces much stronger than her. Mother Nature had taken the very things she loved and made them all weapons, and Ethan was suffering the consequences. Simone was too. They all were. Those tiny, perfect cabins were like paper when confronted by the force of the winds, rain, lightning, and falling pines. Allie held her free hand over her mouth as she saw Jonah emerge unscathed. She felt Simone squeeze her hand back in an acknowledgment of Jonah's presence. Allie exhaled. Just as he walked toward them, a sliver of sunlight pierced through the heavy grayness. Allie had the impulse to wrap her arms around Jonah's neck. Electricity and a need for his touch ran down her spine and through her fingertips. She stopped herself. She remembered the look on Jonah's face when he ran past her seconds after finding her pills. She lowered her eyes as he approached.

"He's in kinda bad shape. I can see where a branch has cut into his leg. I'm pretty sure he has chest injuries from the tree's weight, too." Jonah said to them both. His eyes darted past Allie. "Simone, you might be able to get closer now." Simone nodded and let go of Allie's hand. She stepped across slivers of pine and clusters of needles piled up all around them. Allie drew in an extended deep breath. She folded her long, tan arms across her stomach. She tilted her head.

"Jonah, I can explain." She extended her long neck as she tried to meet his eyes. "I can." Jonah shook his head and moved his eyes everywhere as if hers were chasing his.

"No. I thought we were trying. And now, now I see I was the only one trying, the only one who wanted this." Jonah swallowed back tears. Allie had only seen him fight tears once since she knew him. It was when his father had had a heart attack, and he comforted his mother. Seeing her in pain simply overwhelmed him. Allie hated that her lie had evoked that same response.

"I wanted it, too." She blurted out. "I still do." Jonah stepped back. She wanted to step forward, but she knew he needed that space between them. If she tried to minimize it, Allie feared he'd only create more. Again, the word 'miscarriage' rose from her gut. Allie licked her bottom lip in hopes that it would finally slide out. Jonah took another step back from her. She felt he was a mile away. He was unreachable, and the space would only grow if she didn't throw out something to stop him from leaving. He was floating away from her as if carried by the tide. She needed to toss out a lifeline, something to stop him from sinking or getting carried away from her forever.

"I lost a baby, our baby," Allie said. She drew in another breath and exhaled it slowly. The weight of the last few months dissipated. She straightened her back and relaxed her shoulders. The air was finally light. Jonah made a quick, quiet gasp. His eyes finally met hers. She didn't need to chase them any longer. Then, she noticed it instantly. He was looking at her with the look she had been fearing. He looked at her how she had been looking at herself for months. She was damaged. She failed. He dropped his eyes as Allie stepped closer. "It was when you were gone in April. I had a, a miscarriage." Allie swallowed. Jonah crossed his arms. "I meant to tell you the moment you got off the plane. I did. But, I couldn't."

"April?" His voiced cracked. "April?" his tone rose. He stepped back further. Jonah was out of reach. Allie fought tears. Her chest hurt. Her heart felt as if it had stopped beating altogether. The lightness of the air was quickly replaced with the heaviness she had pushed through for months. The weight that was lifted seconds earlier came crashing back down on her shoulders, her entire body. With his steps back, a sea rushed in. Allie was dizzy and could once again hear ringing in her ears. Through the ringing, she could hear Simone's sobs and the clank of the metal gurney rising into the ambulance. It was all background noise to the sound of Jonah painfully and slowly muttering 'April.' She lost track of how many times he said it, and she couldn't bring herself to interrupt him. She spent months arranging sentences and pleas for this very moment. But, Allie drew a blank. Everything and everyone was gone as she stood alone weighed down by the air and her regrets. Jonah backed away further and faded away behind the wreckage of Simone and Ethan's cabin. She let him go. Allie once again crossed her arms and looked up to the sky as the clouds rolled into the distance and lonely sprinkles darted down, only a trickle now. The beeping of the ambulance, the sounds of Molly and Zack calling for them as they made it to the clearing, and the sound of Jonah's steps growing more faint all swirled around Allie as she let those sprinkles land on her face. She was surrounded by incredible damage and destruction to the clearing, the cabins, and her marriage. The storm had upended everything around her. Pine branches were scattered all around as if the greatest and oldest trees at Moose Pond Lodge had exploded. Her heart broke for those trees, and she was amazed by the force of it all. Everything had been orderly, clean, and predictable an hour earlier.

Allie's eyes scanned the clearing as she searched for something that hadn't been destroyed. She saw a lone willow. It was intact, sturdy, and standing its ground. Its longest branches swayed from the remnants of high winds that had raced through the clearing. It still provided a light green curtain hiding the twists and turns of its intricate branches and trunk. It was tangled, yet all of it coordinated with the rest, top to bottom, to provide protection. The thin slivers of leaves swooshed and hushed each other. It was a gentle presence, yet it had withstood the natural force that destroyed its neighbors. That single weeping willow was unfazed, unbroken. Despite what the world had thrown its way, despite the way everything else around it crashed to the ground below, that willow not only survived, it would thrive. Allie walked towards it as the ambulance drove away from the clearing and Molly and Zack followed behind. She thought of the willows in the Public Garden, the ones that had embraced her and her secrets. That cluster of willows shielded each other. Their roots wove underneath the grass and created a tapestry. Those roots reached deep down and nourished each other, helped each tree stay strong and upright. As Allie stared at that one remaining tree in the clearing, she wondered if she and Jonah would survive the storm she unleashed at their feet. Allie wondered if they'd ever thrive again, grow stronger, nourish each other or ever nourish anything else.

Chapter 7

The Aftermath

Molly

Zack kissed Hannah's forehead as he handed her over to one of the dishwashers.

"You be good for Zoe, okay sweetie?" He said to her. She slid her thumb into her mouth and nodded. "Molly and I are going to follow the ambulance to see how our friend is doing. He got hurt in the storm. It's super important that you stay inside with the pup and listen." The child nodded again. Zack grabbed Molly's hand and rifled in his pockets for his keys with the other. Molly wiped sweat from her forehead as she let him drag her across the floor of the main lodge. Her soaked feet felt like dead weights. Mud was caked on her boots. Her head swirled with the image of Ethan being loaded into an ambulance and Simone looking ghostly white. Molly had never seen that much blood. She was sure she was just as pale as Simone. Molly felt nauseous every time she closed her eyes and pictured Ethan's leg and chest.

"Hey, you okay? You sure you want to head over there?" Zack said as he opened the passenger door of his truck. "It's a mess out there. And, I'm not sure which way the ambulance went. They sure as hell didn't take the main road."

"I have to go. They're my guests. I've got find out how he's doing. I just have to." Molly said. She stared straight ahead as Zack inched the truck onto the main road. Branches were everywhere. The truck zigzagged from one side to the other trying to avoid pine boughs laying every which way. Molly reached over and touched Zack's arm. She held onto the armrest with the other.

"This is just awful, Zack. Just awful."

"Yeah, it's a bad one. I mean, they said it'd be bad, but I didn't expect this. I'm just glad you and Hannah were safe through it." He tapped her hand, which she slid onto his thigh.

"We were safe because of you. I swear, if you hadn't have come back, I would've been left dealing with all that alone, especially getting that call that Ethan needed help. Poor Simone. She already seems frazzled just by being here. I can't imagine what she's feeling in that ambulance." Molly said. She exhaled and sat up straight. "Once the weather service issued that warning, I should've insisted that everyone get to the main lodge. Dammit. I should've made sure no one was in those cabins." She rubbed her forehead.

"Hey, now. You had no idea it would get that bad. No one did. None of what happened is your fault. You hear me?"

"Well, it's kinda hard to believe that. I should've been better prepared. Maybe I should've reinforced the roofs of the cabins. I don't know. But, I'm sure there's something I could've done. Something."

"No, there wasn't anything. You know as well as I do that roof was up to code. Everything there is up to code. You can't do that to yourself. Okay?"

Molly bit her lip. She held on again as Zack swerved out of the way of another cluster of fallen pines. She nodded. She let her mind wander back to her childhood at the lodge. Molly squinted and rubbed her forehead again as she tried to remember if there was ever such a strong storm before. She remembered nights with lightning lighting up the entire ground floor of the lodge. She remembered the cracks of trees falling in the woods, clearing the trails with her father, and wading out into the pond to gather debris that bobbed up and down. But, she didn't remember fear. Molly didn't remember clutching on to her mother or father. She didn't remember any blood, moans, cries, or injuries to family or guests. Maybe she was just too young to grasp the enormity and force of some summer storms in Maine? Or perhaps none were this bad? The electricity was still in the air. She could feel it, almost taste the metallic residue on her lips. Molly was sure she had never been so close to a lightning strike in her life. She raised her hand to her chest and felt her heart beat. That thud in the lodge was unlike anything she had ever felt before. The force and strength of it was awe-inducing and scary at the same time. Molly never felt so helpless as she had in those moments.

"Hey, I'm serious. It's all gonna be alright. He'll be fine. The lodge will be fine. I promise."

"I know. I think I'm just in shock a little. I was never so scared."

"Well, you're fine now. You and Hannah both. I wasn't gonna let anything happen to either of you."

Molly squeezed his thigh and let her head lean on his shoulder as he made his way to the hospital. He was her safety net, her protection from everything the world had thrown at her since he came back to Moose Pond Lodge a year ago. The reasons she played over and over in her head for keeping him at a distance seemed hard for her to recall.

Once the truck came to a stop in the parking lot, Molly and Zack darted toward the emergency room entrance. Suddenly, reality set in that the storm had hit more than Moose Pond Lodge. The beeps of ambulances arriving one after the other then racing off again seemed constant. Molly had never seen so many people gathered in the waiting room and being wheeled from one room to another. Zack let go of her hand.

"I'll go ask the desk where he is, okay?"

Molly nodded. She felt her stomach turn at the thought of seeing Ethan battered and bloody, and also seeing Simone whitewashed and in shock. Zack returned and took her hand as he led her down a hall. Everything echoed, including cries. Molly's eyes peered into each room as they passed. She jerked Zack back as they passed room 108.

"Wait. Come back. That guy, I think I know that guy."

"What? Who?" Zack said as she pulled him back with her. Molly let go of his hand and walked to the threshold of the door. She leaned in as Zack put his hand on her shoulder. "Honey, we gotta find Ethan."

"It's him. It's Martin. The one my mom had an affair with. I know it."

"Come on, Mol." He reached for her hand.

"No, I have to see if it's him and find out why he's here. You go on and find Ethan. Tell them I'm on the way. It's okay. I need to see."

"Okay. But I'm coming back for you if you don't show up in a few minutes."

Molly nodded. Zack let go of her hand as she entered the room. She stood feet from his bed and heard him breathe. Molly took a few slow steps forward.

"Hello? Who's there?" Martin said from the bed. He craned his neck from the sunken pillow.

"Martin? It's me. Molly. Mason and Rosemary's daughter." She stepped forward, so he could see her without straining his neck further. He sunk back down into the crisp white pillow.

"Oh, what are you doing here? Who told you I was here? It's Marty, by the way."

"No one told me. I, I was walking by. A guest at the lodge was hurt during the storm. I'm here to see him and his wife when I happened to spot you." She said as she reached the side of the bed. "Were you hurt out there, too?"

"No, no I wasn't hurt, kid. Have a seat. You look like shit." Molly let a smile slide across her face. "Have a seat." He nodded his head to the chair on the other side of the bed. "Heart attack. I had another heart attack. That's why I'm hooked up to this monitor right now. They're waiting for a room for me. Ambulance got me this morning."

"Oh my God. I'm so sorry. Do you have family coming? How bad is it?"

"Nah, no one's coming. I'll be alright. It's not my first time, you know. I had two last year. The sonsabitches did a stent, got all the blockage cleared. But, I guess I need more maintenance."

"Are you, are you in pain? Do you need anything?"

"No. Just a room away from the chaos out there. That'd be nice." He said with a chuckle. "I figure a week, maybe another stent, and I'll be good to go home, get some peace and quiet." Martin scooted up to sit. "Can you hand me that water, kid?"

Molly stood to hand him the water on the tray at his feet.

"So, your friend, the hurt guest. Is he gonna be okay?" He said after a gulp.

"I'm not sure. Zack, my, my landscaper slash carpenter slash-"

"Boyfriend?"

"Yeah. I guess you could say that. Anyways. Zack is his name. He went to find his room. Ethan Beckwith, the guest, had a tree crash through his cabin. He was pinned under it. Got awful leg and chest wounds."

"Good God. Maine can be a bitch, huh? Those summer storms come outta nowhere. It's like this area gets bored once a few months without a blizzard has passed. She's gotta take all that energy still in the atmosphere, swirl it around, and throw it right at us like a cannonball. I've seen some storms roar in without warning and rip off roofs, topple the greatest pines, and bend metal like nothing. Out of the blue. It's like she gets pissed and turns on us when we least expect it."

"Yeah, that's kinda what happened. It looked awful all morning. Then, it went from winds and clouds to full on tornado-like madness. I guess I'm lucky no one else got hurt. Thank God Zack came back and kept me calm."

"He's a good guy, right? I could see that the few times I lingered around recently."

"Few times?"

"Yeah," Martin said as he took another sip from his straw. "Could you put this back, kid?" Molly took the cup and placed it back on the tray. She sat back down and folded her arms. Molly then leaned forward with her elbows on her knees.

"You were hanging around spying on me?"

"Not spying. Just observing. I was in the lounge here and there before you spoke to me last night. I just felt the need to make sure you were doing okay, with the lodge and all." Martin said. He leaned back and let out a long exhale.

"You okay?"

"Yep. I'm good." He sat up a little more. "Back to this Zack fellow. He good to you? He seems protective, instinctively so."

Molly's eyes widened. She sat up and brushed her hair behind her ears. "Yeah. You could say he's protective. And yes, he's good to me. But, we're keeping things kinda casual. Sorta. He wants to move in, but I think I'm doing fine with the way things are right now." Molly shook her head. "Why am I sharing any of this with you?"

Martin laughed. "I think your dad would've liked him."

"My dad? Wait a minute. You don't get to talk about my dad after what you almost did or did do to my family back then. In fact, you don't get to ask about me at all." Molly folded her arms again. Her heart rate picked up.

She swallowed and wondered why she stopped in his room at all.

"Hey now. Relax there, kid. I'm not trying to upset you. Just because I planned to steal your mom from him doesn't mean I didn't like the guy. He was a helluva guy. I admired him."

"Admired him? You were set to destroy him. I guess you kinda did." Molly swallowed again.

"Well, just for the record, I did admire him. I admired the life he had, the man he was. He was noble, generous, the kind of guy I never was. Maybe that's why I fell for your mom so hard because he had her. He had everything I wanted in life and, well, never had." Martin nodded at the water again. Molly stood and handed it to him. "She was one helluva a woman. I think the way she looked at him was what first attracted me to her."

"What kind of man would admire their love then try to lure her away? To steal it?"

"A desperate man. I guess. A man who had been too stubborn to accept the love of other women, then boom, your mom walks in. I had let others go, and I wasn't about to let another go, too." Martin said. "I was head over heels for her, though. She was something and once she made it clear she was interested, I wasn't gonna lose her."

"She was something all right. I wish you hadn't of told me anything about this, though. It brought up some memories I didn't realize I had."

"I'm sorry, kid. I didn't want to upset you or change how you viewed her or him, honestly. I just, well, I just got to missing her lately, and you're the only person I knew of who knew her too." Martin leaned up more. "Listen. I just felt the need to check up on you, too. I know it doesn't make any sense to you, but I did."

"Yeah, well, I don't need another dad. I'm doing just fine on my own. And quite frankly, how I'm doing and what I do about Zack is none of your business. I don't even know you, Marty. I wish you well and all, but I don't need you to watch over me or dish out fatherly advice." Molly said.

"True, I know you don't need a dad. But hell, kid, if things had gone differently and that accident never happened, who knows, maybe I would've been. Or maybe I would've messed it up with her like I did everyone else." Martin said. "So, listen. You might not need a dad, and I certainly don't need a daughter, but maybe you need a friend."

"A friend huh?" Molly crossed her arms again.

"Yeah, an old guy friend who can tell you when you need a kick in the ass and need to grab your chance at love when it's right in front of your face. A friend who will tell you to cut the bullshit and tell this Zack guy you're in it for the long haul. A friend who will point out that if you let him go, you'll end up alone and ugly like me."

Molly laughed. "You're not ugly. You're actually quite handsome for an old guy. And truth be told, I could use a kick in the ass. Right before that storm, I told Zack he couldn't move in, and he took off. For a moment, I thought I blew it over nothing. I just wanted to prove I could do it all on my own, the lodge, raising my daughter, everything."

"Yeah, stubborn asses like you always gotta prove what the rest of the world knows already. You can do it all on your own, but why choose to if someone good like that guy wants to do it with you?"

Molly knew he was right. She shook her head at the thought of taking the advice of the man who had broken up her parents' marriage and led her father to drown each night away in the lounge. She looked at him lying in that bed and realized he was more than just a guy who fell for her mother. He could be a source of support, a wealth of knowledge she could tap into and drink from, knowledge about her parents and life in general. She felt an odd connection to him. She didn't need a dad, but maybe she needed a dad-figure, a friend who had lived much more. Maybe she needed a sounding board aside from her high school friend, Maxine, and Zack. Maybe letting someone with more life experience in her life wouldn't be a bad thing. Molly had relied on her father's friend and lawyer, Mr. Castille, last summer for guidance, but he was too defensive of her father. He had also known her as a kid and still treated her like one. Carl, her bartender, had his own family to worry about. Martin could be a different connection to her past life, her parents. Also, he could be a friend. *He certainly seemed to need one himself* Molly thought as she realized no one else would be coming to see him.

"You may be on to something, Martin, I mean Marty. And, I think you're right. I could use a friend. I think you could, too." Molly reached over and took his hand. "How would you like a job, too? I need another bartender at the lounge. Carl, my bartender now, wants to cut back on hours to spend time with his grandkids. I really could use the help. Can you make a decent highball?" Molly swallowed.

"Yeah, kid. Maybe in a week or so once I get outta here, I'll stop by and see what I can do."

"Okay. Well, I'll check in on you tomorrow. If you'd like?" She squeezed his hand.

"Yeah. I think that'd be good. Maybe by then, I'll be in a decent room. Now, you get going to see your guest. I'll see you tomorrow, kid." Martin said with a wink. She let go of his hand and gave him a wave as she walked away. Molly felt light again. The storm was gone. Her rage over the truth about her parents and Martin was gone somehow. Her doubts about letting Zack in and being a family with him, Emerson, and Hannah rolled away with the storm. She wanted the life Zack had laid out for them. She wanted the ring in the truck, the puppy nipping at Hannah's dress, both of their girls running up the trails to Moose Pond Lodge. Molly wanted him there every morning and every night, even though she could handle the place alone. She never wanted to stand on that porch and see him drive away again like he had before the storm hit. It had been a year since Zack returned during Allie and Jonah's reception to tell her he was wrong to break up with her and try to reunite with Hannah's mother. Zack said to her that day he knew what he wanted. She was slow to open the door to her heart to him again. She was slow in telling others they were back together for fear that he'd leave on a whim and make her look like a fool. Molly already felt like a failure after her marriage ended and she pulled into Moose Pond Lodge with nothing but Emerson and a desire to rid herself of that place forever. Now a year later as Molly stood in a hospital after a storm and after she nearly wrecked all she and Zack built, Molly could suddenly see clearly. The clouds were gone. The electricity in the air was gone. She didn't need Zack to complete her or to be a success. She didn't need him to hold her hand to keep her from once again drinking her nights away in the lounge as her father had done. She wanted him. Molly wanted all of him and all they could be together as a family at Moose Pond Lodge. He loved that place as much as she did, even though she never expected to fall back in love with it. She never expected any of this, the storm, Zack, or Martin wandering into her life and telling her truths she didn't need or want to know. But, it's what she had now. What she did with the lodge, with her life with Zack, and this newfound friendship with the man who loved her mother was all up to her. The storm had passed, and it was time to move on. She was stronger than she was a year ago. Molly's roots were deep in that place, that spot on earth where she had grown up. As she let those roots run deeper, she grew. She would keep growing. Molly walked the hallway looking for Zack, Ethan, and Simone. She started to pick up her pace. She was anxious to get back to Zack. Whatever damage the storm had done to Ethan, to the resort, to anyone, she'd deal with it. She'd fix it. Molly could fix anything. Having Zack by her side forever would make every bit of the stormy, messy life ahead of them all the sweeter when the sun would come back. That sun would always come back out at Moose Pond Lodge as long as she was there with the ones she loved. Together, as a family, they'd always thrive.

Chapter 8

The Aftermath

Simone

Simone Sterns-Forrester Beckwith leaned back against the cold wall of the sterile hospital room. Zack had asked her a dozen questions. The doctors rattled off information about the status of his leg, pelvis, and the chest wound. She heard the words collapsed lung, internal bleeding, and robotically signed her name to a surgery consent form. While a flurry of movement, beeps, and people spun around the room, all she could do was lean against that wall. It attached her to the reality of the situation, to the severity of it. She exhaled and pulled on the fingers of her right hand with her left. Every time she leaned forward and detached herself from the wall, Simone was transported to those moments in the cabin right after the tree crashed into their tiny world. She had stood there for seconds, or had it been minutes. It was all a blur. However, the one thought that encircled mind in that suspended state was *if he dies, I'll be free.* Her stomach churned as she relived those moments and awful thoughts. Simone pulled her fingers harder until she heard each one crack. It started to hurt. She knew it was nothing compared to what Ethan had felt as he lie under a tree bleeding and gurgling blood from the corners of his mouth.

"Hey, I think I know the answer to this, but you don't happen to have a cigarette on you, do you? Or, in your truck?" She spit out as Zack was still mid-sentence.

"What? Huh? Um, no. I don't smoke. Did you hear me say Molly should be in any minute? When are they taking him up? Wait, you don't smoke. Do you?" Zack asked.

"No, not really. I mean I used to years ago. All the models I ran with did. Oh, Ethan, yes. They're taking him up any second. They've assured me he's going to be just fine. The pelvis might be the most painful part of healing. At least, that's what I think they said." Simone said. She looked past him. "They don't have cigarette machines in hospitals, do they? Of course, they don't."

"Mrs. Beckwith? You can say goodbye real quick then we're taking him to surgery." A nurse said from Ethan's bedside. She was releasing an IV into his arm. "He only has a few minutes before we get him more relaxed."

Simone nodded. She brushed past Zack and stood on the other side of the bed across from the nurse.

"Ethan? Can you hear me?" She whispered down to him. She reached for his hand and gently squeezed. Ethan opened his eyes and moaned. He attempted a smile. He rolled his fingers around her hand. Simone took in a deep breath to suppress the emotions creeping to the surface. "They said you're going to be okay. Okay?" She leaned down and kissed his scraped forehead. "I'm sorry, Ethan. I'm sorry." Simone leaned up as Ethan raised his eyebrows at her. She backed up as the nurse pushed his bed from the wall and towards the door. Another nurse appeared and took the foot of the bed to guide it out of the room. Simone averted her eyes as he passed by. She turned to Zack. "I've got phone calls to make. I'll be in the waiting room after. Thanks for coming and tell Molly thanks, too." She dashed down the hall before Zack could answer.

Simone's head was spinning. She was gasping for air as she pushed the exit doors open with both hands. The doors hit the brick wall on either side. Simone saw a man across the street smoking. She dashed onto the street and ran towards the stranger.

"Can I bum a smoke?" She said as she tried to catch her breath and regain her composure. She gathered her long red hair in her hands and drew the bulk of it to her left side. The man flashed her a slight smile and pulled out a pack from his back pocket.

"Here ya go. You alright? You almost got hit by that car ovah there." He nodded his head at a minivan at the stop sign. Simone saw the driver glare in her direction. It was a woman who looked as frazzled as Simone felt.

"I didn't even notice. Yeah, I'm good. I just need a cigarette to calm my nerves." She said as she took the cigarette to her lips and took a lighter from the stranger's hand. She hadn't smoked in over a decade, except for that April afternoon in New York with Angel. That afternoon, Simone rolled over with the sheet across her chest to touch his arm as he sat up. He had offered her a smoke and without a thought, she took it. When they were lovers, they used to share a few cigarettes after they made love. She stopped smoking the minute her parents picked her up at the police station that rainy night in May. As she sucked on this cigarette, she felt light-headed. Her heart started to race. Simone closed her eyes for a second. The taste filled her mouth. It was instantly dry. She couldn't remember that last time she had water. It had to be after breakfast before the storm hit. She drew in a deeper drag and listened to the sizzle inches from her perfectly pink lips.

Simone remembered the last few moments in the cabin before the tree split their world in two. She remembered telling Ethan that she loved Angel. They had never really talked about him. She wasn't sure she ever said his name out loud to Ethan or anyone after she was picked up and taken from New York, returned to her old life, her old self. *Phone calls to make*, she muttered to herself. She shook her head and put out the cigarette. Simone waved the smoke from her face as she exhaled the last of it. She mouthed a thank you before darting back across the street to the hospital. Simone took out her phone. She knew she needed to call Ethan's parents and his partner at the office. He would most likely be laid up in the hospital longer than they intended to be in Maine. She knew before she dialed and rattled off the details that Ethan's mother would insist on transporting him to Connecticut. Connecticut seemed like a lifetime ago. The last week and a half in Maine had changed so much in her. The storm had. The storm had changed everything. As she promised to keep Ethan's mother updated and to call the second he was out of surgery, she thought of the storm from her childhood. The same fear, uncertainty, loneliness encompassed her outside of the hospital. Her father wasn't going to come around the corner and chastise her for running off and simultaneously ensure her safety. He wasn't going to reassure she'd be fine and explain why hiding under a tree or on the side of a hospital entrance door was the worst idea. She looked at her phone again. She had called everyone she should at a time like this. But, there was one voice she wanted to hear more than anyone else. Angel.

The sun peered out from the last of the storm clouds. Steam rose from the freshly soaked street in front of her. She bowed her head and let her phone barely remain in her hand as her arms hung heavy. Simone had two choices, she thought. She could walk back inside and sit in that waiting room for Ethan. She could rush to be by his side, fawn over him as he regained consciousness. She could be there every step of the way as he was transported to Connecticut and more than likely, sent to a state of the art rehabilitation facility to deal with his broken pelvis. She could cheer him on as he made milestones during a lengthy recovery. She could outfit the house to accommodate anything he needed for the foreseeable future. She could beam with pride as he went back to work, back to normal life. And, she could pray he forgets or overlooks the two minutes of their marriage before that tree fell. They could go back to who they were before that argument before words were thrown around the room. Before she screamed out her love for Angel and declared it was a love he'd never understand. She could do everything in her power for years to prove her gratitude to Ethan. She could love him and continue the happy home and social life they projected to the world. She could redeem herself for those seconds of hesitation before she called for help. She could attain forgiveness for herself for momentarily wishing the worst. Or, Simone could call Angel. She knew there'd be no turning back if she did.

She leaned back on the brick wall and lifted her head to the sky. Simone squinted from the sun. She spotted a weeping willow across the street. The branches hung low and swayed. The sun bounced off the top and raindrops gathered and fell below it even though the rain was long gone. That willow had withstood the storm. It stood alone, unfazed and unsupported. It needed nothing or no one to be strong and steady, and it was still graceful. Simone let a tear fall and didn't bother to wipe it away. She had the urge to crack her knuckles and fidget, but let her arms hang by her side. She drew in a deeper breath and straightened her back. Beads of sweat formed on her nose and forehead as the sun hit her directly. It occurred to her all this time she had been afraid of giving up all she thought she had, the life she carved for herself with Ethan in Greenwich. The idea of walking away from who they all thought she was, who she tried to be for them petrified Simone. Walking away wouldn't be giving up her life, it would be discovering it. Leaving what she knew was the only way to find what she wanted, be who she wanted. The thought *am I strong enough* crept into her mind. "Yes," she muttered to herself. Simone walked across the street and stood near the tree. She let the breeze blow through her hair as she held the phone in front of her. She dialed his number and pressed the phone to her ear as it rang. On the fourth ring, he answered. She heard him take a breath before he whispered her name. She felt as light-headed as she had when she took her first drag of that cigarette minutes earlier.

"Hey. Um, I'll be in New York in a few days."

"For the day again or forever? Honestly, Mona, I couldn't take it if it's just for another afternoon. I don't think I'd survive watching you leave my place again." He said.

"Forever, Angel. Forever." She said as she blinked away tears. "I'll be in touch soon. I've got a few loose ends to tie up here. Then, it's me and you, Mi Alma." She hung up and slid her phone into her back pocket.

Simone ran her fingers through the wispy branches of the willow before she made her way back to the hospital entrance. She found her way into the waiting room where Zack and Molly sat holding hands. Simone told them she would make arrangements with Ethan's mother to transport him home. Molly rubbed her arm and slid her hand into Simone's.

"He's going to be fine. I'm so sorry this happened to you guys. I should've issued a stronger warning and insisted every guest be in the lodge before it hit. I feel sick over this." Molly said. Simone squeezed her hand.

"No, no, Molly. You had no idea it would get that powerful. I hope you're able to repair the cabins, and I'm glad no one else was hurt. I'll, we'll be fine." Simone said.

"Well, we're waiting here with you until we hear he's okay. It's the least we can do."

Simone sunk into a chair as Zack and Molly flanked her on either side. They waited in silence. Simone focused on breathing to avoid panic over the thought of telling Ethan she was leaving, and it was over. Her hands ached from constant wringing. Once the doctor relayed Ethan was in recovery and should be awake in an hour, she insisted Molly and Zack leave. She asked for paper and a pen. Simone shook out her stiff hands and wrote Ethan a letter. She wasn't exactly sure what she wanted to write until the pen hit the page. Then suddenly, words she kept locked away for years started to hit the page with a force she couldn't stop or slow down. She was unleashing a truth, a pent-up and undeniable truth that she didn't even recognize until she let it flow. Simone had lived nearly her entire adult life under the thumb and control of everyone around her, her parents, Ethan, his family, the society groups she belonged to. The only decision she ever made for herself was when she followed Angel to New York. She wrote Ethan the truth. That time in her life wasn't a mistake to hide and never speak of. It wasn't a time or breakdown for everyone to cover-up or gloss over if anyone ever mentioned it. While she respected Ethan and his family, and the life he worked to give her, it was never what she wanted. It was what was necessary. She remembered the words she screamed at him just before the tree fell. She loved Angel. Simone wrote those words. She held the paper in front of her to see them for herself. She promised to work with his family to ensure all his medical needs were met and that his home, his assets, were rightfully signed over to him. She didn't want anything from him. Simone only wanted her freedom. She squinted at that word on the bottom of the page. She smiled as what felt like the weight of the world rose from her bony freckled shoulders. She placed the letter on the table by his bed.

Simone informed the doctor and nurses of his family's contact information and request for transport. She signed forms and let the doctor know how to reach her if something went wrong before Ethan's mother and father arrived later that night or if they couldn't be contacted. While the doctor looked at her with confusion, she never saw things clearer or sounded surer of anything. Simone knew everyone would hate her for leaving before he was awake, for leaving a letter informing him of her plans. She knew there'd be no going back to Greenwich. Her family would bear the brunt of the rumors, once again. But, Simone owned the beach house, her one place of solitude. She had a large amount of cash in her name and a few other assets. In the letter, she told Ethan she wouldn't seek support of any kind if he just signed the papers once they came. She told the truth as simply as she could. What he chose to tell anyone else was his concern, not hers.

A half smile slid across her face as she realized she really didn't care what he, his family, or her family thought in the coming days or even years. Simone was going to be with Angel. That's all she needed and all she cared about. She had suppressed that urge long enough and knew she couldn't bear it a moment longer. Her second of hesitation to get help for Ethan was the lowest and most desperate moment of her life. She was willing if only for a split second to let Ethan die so she could be free rather than stand tall and strong and make her freedom happen herself. She had been a coward and nearly jumped at a cowardly way out. That's not who she ever wanted to be again. None of it was Ethan's fault, and he surely deserved better than she could give him. They both deserved better than what they gave each other. She had worn her parents' name and Ethan's name like a label. Now, she desperately wanted to rip off that label and start a life for herself, being herself, not a Sterns-Forrester or a Beckwith. Simone would never be in anyone's shadow again. She'd refuse to be sheltered from any storm. She could and would stand tall on her own, thrive, and weather anything the world, her family, or Ethan's family could throw at her.

While she was anxious and still a bit scared of what would come once she crawled into the back of a cab, she was certain of one thing. She would now stand strong and honest, chase her freedom, follow where her heart had been all along. She would run confidently and permanently into the arms of the only man she truly loved, Angel. Everything and everyone else be damned.

Chapter 9

The Aftermath

Allie

Allie stood alone in the rain as it tapered to a sprinkle. The birds started to chirp again. They replaced the rumbles and tremendous thuds. She looked up as slivers of sun returned to the clearing. Everything that had upended her world moments ago was gone. The wail of the ambulance, metal clanking of the gurney, moans from Ethan, Simone's cries, and even Jonah muttering "April?" as he backed away from her dissipated. Allie was surrounded by silence, by nature once again. She saw the willow sway and pretended she was in the Public Garden in Boston. For a moment, the gentle breeze and branches flirting with the grass soothed her. But that comfort was replaced by loneliness and emptiness when she let her eyes wander beyond the only tree left standing in the clearing. Breathing in the silence was hard. She missed feeling whole inside. Being alone in the clearing, in the aftermath of the storm, made her notice the emptiness more. The hollowness left from the miscarriage was growing instead of closing. The look on Jonah's face only made the crater in her gut more unbearable.

Allie drew in a deep breath. She needed to find Jonah and try to fix it. She wasn't sure how, but she knew she had to try. He was worth it; they were worth it. It was instinct to pack up and flee anytime her heart was broken. She bolted time and time again without looking back. But, Jonah was different. Jonah grounded her. He anchored her. She grew to need him, turn to him, rely on him when things were out of sorts. Only the one time she needed him most, she had shut him out. Even though it wasn't on purpose and she had no intention of keeping him in the dark forever, enough time had passed that Allie knew she had done grave damage to what they had. She wanted to fix it somehow for him, her, and the family she thought they could still have one day. She didn't know how.

Allie stepped over branches laying in the field and started towards the trail to the lodge. She stepped over puddles of muck filled with pine needles and more branches. The once tranquil trail that provided a never-ending supply of mesmerizing photographs now looked like a bomb had exploded. Debris of every natural form littered the way. Despite the remnants of the storm, the trail was eerily quiet. There was no scurrying, no swaying above her. Everything was still, even the air that had been electric and forceful minutes earlier. Allie slowed her walk. As much as she wanted to find Jonah, spit out a thousand 'I'm sorry's' and feel his arms embrace and protect her, she also wanted the silent protection of the pines and willows that flanked her. She wanted to forget the last few minutes, or months, and stay amongst the woods of Moose Pond Lodge.

Just as she stepped over another cluster of pine boughs, she looked up to see Jonah standing ahead of her. His arms were by his side as he stood firmly at the top of the trail. Allie exhaled and picked up her pace to meet him. She winced when she saw the look in his eyes, a mix of betrayal and devastation. Allie never saw that look before. She reached for his hand. He let her take it. His eyes looked past her as she stepped closer to him.

"Allie. April? Really—" Jonah began.

"I wanted to bear the brunt of this for us, for you. I wanted to be strong enough to deal with this and not break, not break us." Allie said as she reached for his hand.

"You are strong, Allie. But you never gave me a chance to be strong with you, for you."

"No, I'm not as strong as you think. I'm not steady like you. I intended to tell you the second I saw you again, not on the phone. But, when you walked through that gate at Logan, I saw your eyes, the way you look at me. The way you always looked at me. I knew once I said the words out loud, you'd look at me like I saw myself after that Thursday—as broken. It was horrible enough that I saw myself that way, felt that way. I just couldn't bear to break you, too."

"But, Allie, we're a team. We're supposed to go through everything together. You made this your problem, your pain. I don't know what hurts the most—that you lied to me or that you robbed me of grieving this, too. The baby you lost wasn't just yours." Jonah let go of her hand and put both in his pockets. He looked up at the clearing sky. "And, here I was, the last few months, talking about names, colleges, and all that shit. I was wondering why you weren't getting pregnant and wondering if I should make an appointment or suggest you do. I get you want to be strong, but you know what?"

"Wha—" Allie started to say.

"We're intertwined in this life. No one does it all alone, you know? We're supposed to support each other as we grow through this life. I honestly thought that's what we were doing. Growing together. Allie, I don't want there to ever be *your* pain or *your* problem. We're only going to make this work if you see that there's *our* pain, *our* problems. You get that? That's what marriage is." His eyes met hers finally. Allie felt an ache in her heart.

"I guess part of it didn't seem real if I didn't tell you. You know what I'm saying? It was like a roller coaster then a crash, a horrible crash. I ached everywhere for those weeks. I felt empty, gutted like I didn't have a real purpose if I couldn't do this one basic thing. But when you came home, I saw my old self in your eyes. I guess, I guess it was like a reset button of sorts?" Allie reached for his hands again. "Even though I still felt empty and cried for that little one we never got to know, I could look at you and forget for a moment. I could dive into your eyes and pretend to be who I was before the night I stood up from dinner, scraped my plate, and doubled over. Before I felt the bleeding start. I could be the me you loved."

"What was the plan for the long-term? To keep pretending it didn't happen when you were with me? Keep taking the pill forever? Keep tuning me out when I'd blather on about being parents next year at this time?"

"I don't know. All I knew is that I wasn't ready to try again. I needed time to heal. I was trying to avoid hurting you at all cost." Allie stepped directly in front of him. "I wanted to weather this out for the both of us. I wanted to absorb it all, bend with it, and take time to replenish and feel strong again, on my own." She leaned her forehead on his shoulder. He raised his hand to her middle back. "Jonah, I'm sorry." Her shoulders shook as she squeezed her eyes to stop tears.

"I know, Allie. I know. But, I need you to realize you can be stronger by depending on me. We're in this together, you know?" He wrapped his other arm around her and kissed the side of her head. He exhaled deeply into her hair.

Allie dropped her shoulders and let the tears come. She relaxed her legs and leaned on him. She let his arms support her as she cried. She felt drained, empty, weakened. She didn't have the strength anymore to pretend to be strong.

She stepped back and looked at Jonah. She expanded her lungs and drew in the damp air as she wiped her eyes. Allie thought about their wedding a year earlier. She remembered walking towards those eyes. So much had changed in a year, for them both.

He squeezed her hands and drew her closer again. "We can hold off on trying until you're ready, of course." He paused and looked up at the sky again. Another large, heavy cloud was rolling across the treetops. A drop landed on Allie as they both looked up. "But listen. I think I need time to process all of this still. I love you, Alexandra. That'll never change, but this cut deep. I'm going to need time."

"Of course. I understand that, honey. We both still need to heal. We'll get through this. I know we will." Allie said. Jonah stepped away.

"Let's get up to the main lodge before it starts to rain again." He grabbed her hand as they made it to the top of the trail. He led her up the steps of the main lodge right before the sky opened again. Before Allie could reach for the door, Jonah pulled her back to face him. "I think we should cut this trip short. Or, I should maybe."

"What? And go back home a few days early? I mean, sure, I can get some stuff done at home before I need to be back at the paper. I guess." Allie said.

"No, I mean I'm going alone for a few days," Jonah said. The words were slow. They hovered above Allie's head.

"Wait. What? Like a few days apart?" Her voiced cracked. "Jonah, this is our first anniversary. It's our trip, not yours or mine alone. You just said we're in this together. Me and you. Taking a few days apart isn't what I want. I don't think it's what we need." Her eyes welled up. "Seriously, Jonah? You just said we need to nourish and support each other, and all that. I'm not staying here alone, and I'm not heading home without you." Allie's hands shook. She felt a tingling in her arms and legs as if the electricity that had been in the air was bubbling up in her gut and getting ready to burst from her fingertips. She tried to slow her heart rate, her pulse, and her emotions. Allie was suddenly dizzy. She held her hand to her forehead and wished for a wave of calm. "Jonah, please, please. Lets—"

"What, Allie? Deal with this together right here and now? You didn't think so in April. This is all new to me. I need to leave and process this. I really think that's best right now, for me and you. For us."

Allie's head was spinning. She felt as if she was falling, losing her ability to control herself, control anything around her. She drew in a deep breath as Jonah steadied her and held her back to look into her eyes. She let her eyes meet his. She could see he wasn't trying to shut her out or punish her. He wasn't angry. He was just different. Allie's hands tensed. She felt as if she was grasping at nothing and everything all at once. She stood bare like a tree whose branches had snapped, stripped of needles, leaves, or even bark, jagged and splintered. Allie wanted to reach into the nothingness, the space between her and Jonah and reattach all that lay at their feet. She wanted to glue the pieces back together for both of them. Even more so than the moment he scooped those pills from the cabin bathroom floor, Allie wondered if she could repair what she had broken between them.

Allie sunk into the rocking chair, the very rocking chair she sat on after their wedding. Once her body melted into the wooden frame, she instinctively rocked slightly. The sights, smells, and pure bliss of that day overwhelmed her.

"Why can't we go back to last year at this time, Jonah? Remember sitting here, watching all the kids run around, listening to the music, the cool breeze, the lights on that gazebo. Remember that cake? My god that was a great cake, Jonah. That was a perfect day. Why can't we go back to that day and start over?" Allie rocked harder as she gripped the arms of the chair. Jonah sat in the chair next to her.

"Yeah, that cake was perfection, babe." He said as he sat next to her looking at the gazebo.

"Well. Let's start tomorrow. We'll go hiking, fishing, I'll take pictures, and we'll make love all night. Then, we can go home, regroup, and move forward." She threw every reason at him she could think of to make him stay. She swallowed a new lump in her throat after each one. Allie felt her stomach churn. Her hands shook as she reached over to grasp his arm. She sunk her nails into his skin, afraid if she let go, he'd disappear like the baby did.

Jonah reached over and peeled her hand from his arm. Tears burst from her eyes as she stared straight ahead. Allie stopped rocking. He rose from the chair and stood next to her.

"Tell me, Jonah, tell me we'll get back to where we were. Tell me we can fix this."

"I want to, Allie. I really want to. I need to go."

"But, I need you to stay." She said through tears. He reached down and touched her shoulder.

"Well, it looks like we need two different things right now." He pushed his hands in his pockets. "You stay here. I know you'll be fine hanging out with Molly, checking on Simone and Ethan. You'll have the chance to explore the woods, the lake, and take the pictures you want. But, I need to go, and I need to go alone."

"Why do I feel like I'm gonna lose you if you go without me." She wiped her eyes. "Please, Jonah. We need to deal with this together." Allie said. She wiped her nose. Allie stood up in between Jonah and gazebo across the lawn.

"Really, Allie? Really? Do we? Where was that attitude in April? Damnit. You don't get to dictate this like everything else. You kept the loss of a child from me, the loss of my child. Then, you started taking the pill and hid that from me, too. Jesus, Allie. My head is spinning thinking of the last few months and how you hid all of this from me." Jonah tried to lower his voice. "This isn't your call. Not this time. Don't you get that? You don't get to tell me how I should, or we should go about dealing with this." Jonah turned his back to her then spun around to face her again. "I'm trying so hard right now not to lose it. I'm not asking you to agree to stay while I go. I'm not even asking anymore if you get why. I'm telling you what I need. And that's what I'm going to do." Jonah let out a groan and looked up at the ceiling of the porch. "Listen. I'm calling for a car and heading down to Hampton. My uncle is there this month and has a charter boat. I'll go out and do some deep-sea fishing for a few days and then I'll head back to Boston."

"Please stay. I'm scared." Allie said as she tried to meet his eyes.

"Scared of what?" Jonah snapped.

"I'm scared if you go, this emptiness in me will grow. This distance will grow. And, I'm scared you'll never come back, come back to me." Allie looked down again.

"I'm going to the cabin to pack up what I can. Stay here, please. Just stay here."

"Then what? You'll leave? And, we'll meet back up at home at the end of the week?"

"I don't know, Allie. The more I stand here, the more unsure I am of anything right now. I'm not trying to hurt you or punish you. I just, I've got get out of Maine and away from you right now." Jonah stepped off the porch and out into the drizzle that lingered once again. He turned and looked at Allie. She could see he was tearing up.

"I'm sorry, Jonah. You know that don't you? Please tell me you know that?"

He nodded. "I'll text once I get to Hampton and let you know I made it and found my Uncle."

Allie started to step forward. She fought the urge to throw herself at him full force, tackle him to the ground, and pin him under her forever. She knew she couldn't. It wouldn't make a difference. Jonah was leaving, and Allie knew there was nothing she could do to stop him. Jonah turned and started to walk towards the trail. A thousand words jumbled and fought for space in her mouth. Air didn't come in or out. She was suspended, paralyzed in the moments as he got further and further away. Regrets bubbled up, and she tasted the bitterness mixed with her salty tears. She walked down the steps of the porch and let the drizzle mist over her entire body. Allie thought if she had told him immediately, yelled out in the airport, he would've understood. He would've comforted her and understood why she wanted to stop trying for a while. Why didn't she just tell him? Allie wondered if there was something inherently wrong with her, with them. He was right. She robbed him of grieving, too. Between the miscarriage, arguments and snide remarks about moving to the suburbs, their changing career paths, and her constant need for escape, maybe there were underlying issues she refused to see or share? Maybe Jonah was right. Time apart was what they needed, and perhaps, they needed more than just a few days.

The urge to follow Jonah dissipated. She needed to step aside. She wanted to step aside, at least for the moment. Maybe, she thought, that's what this marriage was supposed to be—taking turns taking the lead, taking time alone to heal before healing together, letting Jonah go when he needed to go and trusting he'd come back. Allie glanced around at the damage, the fallen trees, scattered branches. So much damage had unfolded over the last few hours. One storm, one moment, one decision had uprooted everything in her life. For the first time since she met Jonah, the surety of 'them' was in doubt. She wasn't in the lead. She wasn't holding the reins of their relationship, their future. Allie had always believed they were unbreakable simply because she decided that's who they'd be—the unbreakable couple. They could and would survive anything. Their life and marriage would be them against the world. Without warning, all that confidence slipped from her fingertips and puddled at her feet as she stood in front of Moose Pond Lodge. Maybe there were battles they couldn't survive? Maybe every fight or disagreement wouldn't result in a stronger union, a stronger tree with intertwined roots? Maybe, Allie feared, one storm could be fierce enough to do more than bend them. Maybe they could break. Maybe they had. There was no guarantee they'd thrive, grow, or even survive this storm. The worst part about this realization was the fact that Allie knew there was nothing she could do about it now. Either they'd heal, grow, and thrive in the sun and rain again. Or, maybe they'd wither because the broken branches were too much for them to survive. After all, there are storms tragic enough to kill even the strongest and most resolute willows.

Chapter 10

Molly

Molly slid into the passenger side of Zack's truck. She squinted as the sun peeked through the storm clouds that were left. A slight mist covered the truck. She slammed the door closed and pulled her seatbelt.

"I really miss Emerson, but I'm so glad she was with her father for this storm. It'll be impossible to clean it all up before she flies home from Nashville though." She sighed. "Zack, as much I want to get home, I gotta tell you, I'm scared to see how bad the damage is."

Zack started the truck and tapped her thigh before putting it in gear. "Honey, it's gonna be okay. We'll repair it all, rebuild stuff, just like last summer when you took this place over." He pulled out of the hospital parking lot. "I'm just glad to hear Ethan is going to be okay. Simone still seems in shock, though."

"Yeah. She seemed pretty rattled and by much more than just his injuries. Trust me. There's definitely a story to that one." Molly said as she gazed out the window. "God, Zack. Did you see those cabins though? The roofs of what? Three, maybe four were torn to shreds. The trail. We worked so hard on that trail last summer. Who knows what damage there is to the roof of the lodge."

"We'll do what we did before. We'll rebuild like I said."

"What would I do without you?" Molly said as Zack squeezed her thigh again. "Seriously? I can't imagine not having your help. And honestly, I don't even deserve it the way I've been acting." Molly started to tear up.

"Hey, hey, no. Don't do that. I'm not going anywhere." Zack said as he swerved around a branch in the road.

"I wouldn't blame you if you did. I'm sorry I've been so obnoxious. You asked to move in with me, and I exploded like you were leaving me instead. I'm just all mixed up I guess. I wouldn't blame you if you just bolted. You and Hannah both." Molly wiped her eyes. Zack pulled over on the side of the road. He put the truck in park.

"Hey there. There's nothing to be sorry or upset about. I was pushing. I've been pushing. It just seems like you've been in my life, my mind forever. But, I gotta remember it's only been a year since you got divorced from Kenny and made a home here. A year. That's not much time to get yourself settled." Zack turned toward her and took her hand. "Plus, in the middle of that divorce and your dad's death, we went in full throttle. I mean full throttle. Then to top that off, I go and break up with you out of the blue after Hannah's accident. I put you through hell by thinking I should give Hannah's mom another chance just when you and I were making a go of it. I'm lucky you took me back when I showed up during Allie and Jonah's wedding."

Molly cracked a smile. "Oh stop. You knew I'd take you back and try again."

"No, Molly. I didn't, and you didn't have to let me walk up to that porch and ask for another shot at this. Seriously. I should be grateful we're together and making this work with the kids and all, and now a dog. All you asked of me is to take this slow, let you regroup and prove you could make a go of life here on your own. And, well, I didn't do that. I went full throttle again. I'm gonna back off. Okay? So, don't worry about me moving in or anything. We can keep things as they are for as long as you need to."

"I love you, Zack, but-"

"I know you do. That's all I need to know. Okay?" Zack started the truck. "Now, we gotta get back and check on Hannah and the nameless puppy I got. What have I done there, getting a dog when I can barely keep up with that kid?" He said with a laugh. Molly laughed, too.

"I offered Martin a job bartending. Carl said he wants some time off because of stuff with his kids and grandkids, and I think I could use someone else to help out in the lounge at least." Molly said. She stared straight ahead, knowing the idea sounded crazy out loud.

"A job for the guy whose very existence had you rattled and questioning everything, what? Just yesterday?" Zack said. He kept glancing at her and the road as he slowly veered away from various branches.

"Yeah. I know. I just, something about talking to Marty, seeing him in that hospital bed, touching his hand. Zack, he doesn't have anyone. There's no one out there for him." Molly felt her heart sink a little remembering how frail he looked. "I can't explain it. It was just a feeling, an instinct that I wanted to be around him, get to know him." She brushed her short blonde hair from her eyes and behind her ear. Molly turned to Zack. "Maybe it's as simple as thinking he's the last connection to my parents? Maybe not. I'm not sure why or what it is. But the words 'come bartend at the lounge' just fell out of my mouth."

"Well, you can always fire him if it doesn't pan out like you want."

"I'm not even sure what I think will pan out about it. Or, what I want to pan out about it. Maybe I'm just torturing myself? Looking for more reasons to be filled with angst about my mom dying, dad being an alcoholic, or not. Who knows. Maybe I need to give him the chance I didn't give my dad."

"Maybe he won't disappoint you."

"Maybe that's it," Molly said as she leaned forward. The truck inched up the driveway to the main lodge. She spotted shingles laying around the driveway and gazebo. Pots she moved for protection still managed to lay upended at the foot of the gazebo. The lights dangled from the entrance. Molly bit her bottom lip. *I forgot to take down the lights.* Her eyes scanned the lounge entrance on the side. Debris seemingly from every corner of Maine was strewn about.

"It looks like, like chaos." After the words escaped her lips, Molly let out a long exhale. Zack turned off the truck. They both stepped out. Molly immediately felt off-kilter. She wanted to close her eyes and not let another sight of the storm enter her memory. Zack walked around the took her hand. She heard him say over and over again, "It can all be fixed." She knew he was right, but it didn't alleviate the weight bearing down on her shoulders. It was the same sinking feeling she had when she pulled into Moose Pond Lodge over a year ago, right after the death of her father. She drew in another deep breath and started to walk towards the porch when a car backed up and started toward the driveway. Jonah was in the back seat. He gave them both a slight wave before averting his eyes. Molly and Zack waved back in confusion. Molly thought he looked broken.

"Where's he going?" Molly said. Zack shrugged his shoulders.

"I don't know. But wherever it is, he's got his luggage with him."

As they climbed the porch steps, the door flung open. Hannah and her new puppy raced to Zack's waiting arms. He scooped up his daughter and covered her face in kisses until she squirmed from his grasp. "You okay, kiddo?"

"Yep, daddy. I'm fine. Sunshine!" She pointed behind them. "See it? The sun is winking at us finally." Zack and Molly turned around to see the sunlight pierce through the gray clouds. The beam appeared to hit Hannah directly as Zack let her slide down to her feet. "Sunshine!" she yelled again as the puppy pulled on her clothes, nearly dragging her down the porch steps. Zack picked up the dog.

"Yep, that storm is gone, and the sunshine is back." Zack patted Hannah on the head. "You think of a name for this guy while we were at the hospital checking on our friends?"

"Hmm," Hannah said as she placed her tiny hands on her tiny hips. She bobbled back and forth looking up at Zack as he calmed the wild puppy. "Sunshine!" she squealed. "Sunshine the dog." A smile grew across her tanned face as she moved her brown curls from her happy eyes. Molly laughed.

"Sunshine it is!" Zack yelled. Molly wanted to wrap the two of them in her arms, then swallow them whole. Throughout the year, she had come to love Hannah like her own. Molly couldn't imagine not having the two of them in her life forever. She folded her arms and giggled at Hannah jumping as high as she could to reach the puppy in Zack's arms.

"Listen, I'm pretty sure everything is safe for you to stay here tonight, okay? I'm gonna take Hannah home and tuck these two into bed early. It's been a long day for her and this crazy dog, too."

"Sunshine. His name is Sunshine, Daddy." Hannah said. He nodded at her and patted her head again.

"Okay. Yeah, I think I'll do a quick walk down to the trail to the clearing, just to get a glimpse of how bad it is. Then, I'll turn in early, too."

"You don't need to walk down there now. It can wait till tomorrow. All of it can wait until tomorrow, honey."

"I know. I'm not getting distressed about it, honestly. I just need to see it with my own eyes." Molly said as Zack leaned down and kissed her forehead.

"Okay. Just remember what I said. It's all fixable. We're okay. The guests are okay. Ethan will be okay, too."

"Speaking of guests, I should find Allie since we saw Jonah leaving. It didn't look like a good situation."

Zack kissed her again then released the puppy. Hannah pulled at Molly's shirt and puckered her tiny lips. She closed her big brown eyes waiting for a kiss goodbye. Molly's heart melted as it did every time Hannah kissed her. She leaned down, and her lips met the child's. Hannah's lips were warm and tasted like a cherry lollipop. Hannah made a loud smack with her lips and giggled. Molly was amazed by her innocence. Just hours earlier, the most intense storm of her little life rolled through and made her shake in Molly and Zack's arms. She was surely frightened while Zack and Molly were at the hospital. Now, she was her bouncy, bubbly self wholly immersed in her new dog, just as a little five-year-old should be.

Molly watched Hannah bounce down the porch steps to follow the dog to the truck. Zack leaned in for one more quick kiss.

"Can you believe she'll be starting kindergarten?" Zack said as he turned to follow his daughter. Molly laughed.

"She's such a doll baby still. I love her." Molly said. Zack turned back around and looked at Molly as he made it to the last step.

"I know you do." He winked at her and dashed to the truck to lift Sunshine and Hannah inside. Hannah wildly waved as they drove past.

Molly unlocked her arms and decided to head toward the trail. She meandered around branches and marveled at the silence. There had been so much noise, chaos earlier. There was still a slight breeze. The hairs on her arm rose, telling her there was still electricity in the air. As she took in the damage done to the nature path she walked her whole life, Molly searched her memories for a storm that compared. She remembered waking in the middle of the night to cracks of thunder and booms that shook the window. She remembered snow drifts and blizzards that kept them trapped for days without electricity and the fireplace as their only source of heat. Molly squinted when she remembered one storm that raced across the summer sky as she swam in Moose Pond as a teenager. She spent more time staring at the

approaching rain clouds and daring her best friend Maxine
to stay in the water with her than she did running to hide
or worrying about the danger. Molly shook her head
thinking she was only a few years older than Emerson
when she stupidly dared Mother Nature to show her
who's boss. She hoped Emerson had more sense than she
did as a kid. But, she couldn't remember fear like she felt
hours ago. She couldn't remember a pain in her chest wall
with each thud of thunder or ever burrowing her face into
the chest of her dad or any other man. Today was
different. Then, she pictured the scene and chaos of Ethan
being taken away by ambulance. The blood on his clothes,
face, and on the branches that held him down. The look on
Simone's face—a stone white, frozen look of fear. The
panicked look on Allie and Jonah's face as they tried to
move more branches as the emergency crew cut the
largest from over the top of Ethan. The uncertainty of
everyone's fate.

Molly rubbed her arms to dispel the chills as she
rounded the corner to the clearing. She stopped and
gasped as she saw the changes, the damage, all in silence.
Three cabins had severe roof and structural damage. Of
the ones that remained, the flower boxes, rocking chairs,
and pots of annuals looked as if a dozen mini-tornados
swirled through. Petals and roots of flowers she spent
weeks planting, and dead-heading were chewed up and
spit out by mother nature's wrath. Her heart raced as she
wandered in a circle, taking it all in. Zack's words kept
playing in her head. *It can all be fixed.* They could and
would fix it together, just as they had done last year when
she worked tirelessly to get the crumbling resort ready for
the season. Her father had left behind chaos, a wrath of
sorts, for her and Zack to repair. Back then, she found
comfort in the effort, the end result. She found solace in

the aftermath. She took that wreckage and turned it into a thing of beauty and order. With Zack's help and reassurance, Moose Pond Lodge could again be a thing of beauty. Molly looked up at a clear sky, which only hours ago looked like it would swallow up everything she held dear. She saw calm and felt hope warming her face once again. She couldn't glue branches back on the trees. She couldn't put the petals back on the flowers. But, she could begin the work of making the cabins and trails at Moose Pond Lodge beautiful and peaceful again starting tomorrow.

Molly realized night would be covering the lodge like a blanket soon. She walked back the trail and to the lounge. Molly flipped on the light and was surprised to see Allie alone at the barstool looking down at her folded hands.

"Hey, you. You okay? Where was Jonah heading earlier?" Molly said as the screen door slammed and startled Allie. "Sorry."

"I'm okay. Jonah is gone." Allie said. Molly could tell she was fighting tears that waited just behind her eyes. Molly walked behind the bar.

"I didn't expect anyone to be in here. Sorry, I scared you. What do you mean gone? Did he find another place for you guys to stay? I told you I have plenty of rooms here in the main lodge for everyone." She grabbed a glass and filled it with seltzer. "I'm parched. You want a beer or anything?"

"Yeah, please. He decided to head to Hampton, catch a ride on his uncle's charter boat, and well, spend the rest of our anniversary vacation apart." Allie exhaled as if she was deflating before Molly's eyes.

"Apart?" Molly slid a drink in front of her. After a few nights of hanging out in the lounge after dinner, Molly knew she liked. "Why? Allie, what happened?"

"Well, long story short. I told him about the miscarriage." Allie said looking at the beer in front of her. Molly went around the bar and sat next to Allie. Molly's heart ached as she listened to Allie explain the pills, the fears, and the anger she saw in Jonah's eyes.

"Molly, I'm afraid he'll never...." Allie's once commanding and self-assured voice trailed off into a crackle of tears. Molly wrapped her arm around her and drew Allie's head to her shoulder.

"I'm so sorry, Allie. What are you gonna do? Stay here a few days then drive home?" Molly asked. Allie shook her head as she sat up and reached for a bar napkin. She blew her nose with great force and slumped her shoulders. Allie tucked her long black hair behind her ears.

"Tomorrow, I'm going to take pictures of the sun and willows, the water, and anywhere else that makes me feel a little bit better about all of this." She sipped her beer more. Molly noticed she was half done with it.

"That's a good idea. Zack and I are going to clean up what we can and hopefully get a crew in here to fix the cabins. Everything seems to be shambles, but I know it'll look better in the morning. Maybe all of this with Jonah will look better in the morning, too?"

"I hope you're right."

"Well, Moose Pond Lodge isn't the only thing I've got to fix around here."

"What do you mean?" Allie asked as she blew her nose again.

"I had a major falling out with Zack before the storm. Asked him to back off and said I didn't want him to move in."

"Oh, no. Did you guys—"

"No, we didn't break up or anything. In fact, on the way back here from the hospital, he actually agreed with me. About keeping things light and casual like we've done since last summer."

"So, what's the problem then, Molly?"

"Well, after the storm, seeing what happened to Ethan, and just how scared I was until he grabbed me close, I think keeping it light isn't what I want anymore."

Molly got up and walked to the other side of the bar. She got another beer for Allie. "I might have blown my shot at having this thing with him be something more. I finally got what I wanted from him, and well, it's not what I think I want now."

"You won't know until you take a shot at telling him what you want now. I guess." Allie drank the rest of her bottle and immediately started on the next. Molly warned her to slow down a little. Allie shrugged. "Enough of our problems with men and our stupid mistakes. New subject. What happened to Simone and where did she take off to?" Allie said before another long swig. Molly smiled.

"I don't know. Like I told Zack, there's definitely a story with her."

"Yeah. Leaving Ethan at the hospital and taking off from here. Crazy." Allie huffed. "Then again, my husband left right after we saw her head out."

"Allie, that's different," Molly said even though she wasn't so sure if it was.

"I guess I'll know in a few days. That storm, Molly, that storm seemed to wreck a whole lot more than just your home. You know?"

"Yeah, I know."

After Allie enjoyed another beer, Molly offered to walk her down the hall to the room she'd sleep in because of damage to the cabins. She helped Allie slide into the bed and pulled the quilt out from under her.

"This is one of your mom's quilts, like the one you gave me for my wedding last year, right?" Allie mumbled.

"Yes, yes, it is." Molly lifted Allie's foot from on top of the quilt and unlaced her boots. "They are all I have of her, sort of."

"Sort of?" Allie said as she pulled at one foot and Molly pulled at the other.

"I invited Martin to work here. The guy she had the affair with, remember?"

"Wow, you really want to open old wounds, keep them open, and pour a shit-ton of salt into them, too. Huh?" Allie slurred. Molly let out a laugh and huff at the same time.

"I'm not sure. I just felt compelled to get to know him more."

Allie leaned back and pulled the quilt close to her chest. She flopped her arms on either side of her stomach.

"Well, good luck with that, Molly. Good luck." She closed her eyes.

"Thanks. I'm not sure what I'm doing. But, apparently, I don't need to be sure all of the time." Molly said. She realized Allie was fading away into a drunken sleep. Molly smiled at her and walked to the door. She glanced back at Allie again. Even though she only knew Allie from her wedding last summer, something about Allie's presence made Molly feel strong, more capable, resilient in a way. Molly realized she fed off Allie's air of confidence, self-assuredness, even when Allie was a woman filled with doubts and fears about the status of her marriage. There was something Molly wanted to absorb more of when it came to Allie. She wanted to know her better, deeper, and forever. Molly closed the door and made her way to her bedroom. It seemed like a lifetime had passed since she left in the morning. So much had changed, had happened to them all. Molly changed and crawled into her parent's old bed, the bed where she spent so many nights with Zack in the last year. She closed her eyes knowing tomorrow would be okay. He'd be back to help, and everything would fall back into place.

Molly woke to the sight of Zack above her. He was smiling and dressed to work. She smiled back at him and remembered a dream she had. She was chasing him down the trail and into the water. Suddenly, in her dream, he took flight above her, dressed in a ridiculous white suit. He reached his hands down and grabbed her to lift her in the air. Together they swirled above the pond, laughing. He kept telling her she could let go of his hands. At first, she thought she'd fall if she did. Zack let go of her and gave her a slight push away. For a moment, she panicked. Then realized she was floating alongside him. They spun and even though she was dizzy, Molly couldn't stop smiling, laughing, and floating with him.

"What are you smiling at, goofball?" Zack said as she tapped her foot.

"Oh, I had a dream about you. That's all."

"What kind of dream?" Zack said as he winked at her. "If it's the kind I had about you, we don't have time for that this morning. Get up. I already made breakfast and let you sleep. Now, it's time to get to work." Zack flashed her the same smile as in her dream.

After a quick shower, breakfast, and checking in with Allie and the other remaining guests, Molly followed Zack outside to the porch.

"I brought out my four-wheeler to start dragging branches from the trail. No sense having any contractors come in to fix cabins if they can't drive the trail." She hopped on the back, and they began the work of moving what they could by hand and tying and dragging what they couldn't.

Molly was dripping in sweat by the time the sun was straight overhead. Zack had removed his shirt hours ago. She watched him. Not just amazed at his physique, but his stamina when working on the trails with her. She could tell with every grunt and ripple of biceps and triceps that Zack truly gave Moose Pond Lodge his all when he helped her. Molly realized he loved this land and the resort as much as she did.

The branches grew heavier as they made it closer to the end of the trail. Molly fought the clusters of needles and cones with her giant metal rake. She dragged piles to the edge of the trail, unveiling sand that had led the way just 24 hours earlier. One storm had destroyed so much. But, so much wasn't broken, she kept reminding herself. The giant willow in the clearing, the weeping willow that tickled the top of one cabin still swayed with the same gentleness as the day before. It was stronger than the rest. It was steadfast in its ability to dig in deep, keep it's roots intact, and adjust to the winds and rain. It bent with what the world threw at it. It survived it all. It would continue to grow and thrive. Molly got lost in the swaying branches when Zack broke her spell.

"Mol? I'm gonna take a dip in the pond quick. I need to cool down." She glanced at him as he walked away toward the sandy beach still left along Moose Pond. She watched him slide off his shoes and shorts. Molly slowly walked his way, debating taking a dip herself. She watched him go under, re-emerge, and then float on his back. Molly remembered the first time they made love after floating in the pond. The sand stuck to her hands and legs, the smell of his sweat as she drank him in and he drank her in. Molly wanted nothing more than to always stand on the edge of that pond and watch him. The way he floated above the water she loved all her life. The way he made everything calm, rippling and hypnotic. Molly could stare at him forever.

Zack splashed his arms on top of the water and stood upright. He walked out of the water toward his clothes. Molly ran up to him before he could reach down. She knelt on her knees and grabbed both his hands. He flinched in surprise.

"Zack Preston. I don't need a damn ring in your truck. I don't need to slow down, take things casual, or any of that shit I said all year. I just need you, and this place, and our girls. That's it. I just need us. Zack, marry me?" The words poured out of her mouth before she even knew what she was saying. Zack's eyes widened. "Marry me?" She blurted out again as she started to shiver all over. She felt as if she would burst if he didn't say anything soon. Zack pulled her to her feet. He smiled a grin that could've swallowed the world as he pulled her closer.

"Dammit, woman. I thought you'd never ask." Zack said as he leaned down and kissed her.

Molly's feet left the ground as he enveloped her. She was floating. They were floating. Even with roots that ran deep under the ground, the trail, the cabins, and main lodge. Even with branches that had been bent and strained as far as they could withstand. Even with seeing everything else around them crumble. They floated above it all, stronger as one. Unbreakable together.

Chapter 11

One Year Later

Molly looked in the mirror as she smoothed the front of her dress. Wisps of her short blonde hair protruded from the crown of daisies on her head. She noticed dirt stains around her cuticles even after scrubbing her hands night and day. Even with pale pink nail polish, she had the hands of a landscaper the last two springs and summers. She laughed thinking she'd soon be a landscaper's wife, so no use expecting clean hands again. Molly rolled her eyes thinking of all the times Zack told her to wear gloves. She hadn't minded the sweat, dirt, and tears it took to keep Moose Pond Lodge beautiful the last two years. She wasn't about to start wearing gloves now even if it was her wedding day.

Thoughts of her mother and father were never far from her heart and mind. Molly closed her eyes and pretended they were on either side of her. She swayed slightly. She smiled as a warmth ran up her bare arms and neck. She exhaled a longing for them Molly hadn't felt in a long time. She swayed a little more and slowly opened her eyes. Molly smiled as one tear rose to blur her vision. They were with her. Mason and Rosemary were on either side of her and always would be.

Emerson and Hannah broke her trance. They burst into Molly's bedroom and flanked her on either side, just as she pictured her parents would do if they could. Emerson was giggling. She had grown nearly a foot in the two years they lived in Maine. While Molly was only five and a half feet, Kenny was tall. Emerson took after his side, except she had Molly's smile and blue eyes. Molly knew Emerson was on her way to becoming a beautiful young woman, complete with an adventurous streak. Hannah tugged at her dress. She had also grown. Her curly brown hair was in a wrap around braid to match Emerson's, who Hannah had already started calling her big sister. They both wore matching gold-colored dresses with roses embroidered around the neckline. Emerson picked them. Naturally, if Emerson thought the bridesmaid and flower girl dresses were a cool choice, Hannah agreed.

"Where's your basket of flowers, sweetie?" Molly asked Hannah.

"I left them by the fireplace with Sunshine. He said he'd guard 'em." She said. Hannah placed her hands on her hips and rocked back and forth as she watched herself in the mirror. "I can't wait till we can dance in the gazebo. You said I could dance on stage, right Molly?"

"Of course, you can. You can dance anywhere you want, anytime you want. This isn't just mine and your dad's wedding. It's all of us, getting married and becoming a family."

"I can't wait," Hannah said. "Can I have lipstick, too?" She asked. Her six-year-old mind fluttered from one thing to the next without rhyme, reason, or warning. Molly loved that about Hannah and missed it about Emerson. While extraordinarily articulate and well-adjusted, Emerson was much more serious than Molly remembered being at that age. Molly considered her an old soul who knew the way through this life of hers without needing much direction from Molly, Kenny, or Zack, or anyone else for that matter.

"Yep. You can have some of mine. It's okay, right Mom?" Emerson said as she rummaged through her gold clutch. Molly nodded. As Emerson ran a light coat of shiny mauve lipstick across the little girl's lips, Maxine opened the bedroom door.

"Oh my God. You look amazing. The way that dress hangs on you is gorgeous. It's like it was made for you, Mol." Maxine tapped the top of Hannah's head and winked at her as she slid next to her childhood best friend. "Wow. When you first came back to town two years ago, I can't say I saw this coming."

"I didn't either. I didn't plan on staying more than a few days. Man, everything changed in a blink. I'm sure glad it did, though. There's nowhere else I'd rather unexpectedly end up." Molly said with a slight laugh. "And, you know what the best part about ending up back here has been, besides Zack and getting to be family to this little cutie?" Molly said as she wrinkled her nose at Hannah, who had jumped up on the bed and was watching them in the mirror.

"What?" Maxine asked as she tried to smooth some of the wisps of hair on Molly's head.

"I got to be best friends with my best friend again. I can't imagine doing this without you, doing anything without you." Molly felt a lump in her throat as she saw Maxine's eyes water.

"Yeah, well, someone has to look out for you. God knows you can't take care of yourself. Thankfully Zack is around to share the load of handling you." Maxine winked and nudged Molly with her elbow. "Come on, there's a guy in a nice black suit standing at the front of that gazebo, and he's looking for a bride."

Molly nodded and smoothed the ivory silk strapless gown again. Truth be told, she didn't care about the wrinkles if there were any. She didn't care much about her hair, nails, or makeup. She just wanted to be in front of Zack Preston with Emerson and Hannah by her side. She wanted to start her life with that man.

"I'll tell them to start the music, okay?" Maxine said as she went to the door.

"Maxine, wait."

"What?"

"Thank you. Thank you for everything. I know you did so much of this behind the scenes. You've always done so much for me behind the scenes. I was awful the years I was away, then awful when I first got back. I just—"

"Shut up. Don't get me all teary. I paid a lot for these lashes and foundation. You'll ruin it if you keep talking." Maxine said. She slid out the door and down the hall. Molly felt as if her heart would burst through her chest as she thought how lucky she was. She knew Maxine was waiting by the fireplace and was most certainly wiping away tears herself.

"Okay, girls. Let's be ready." Molly said as Hannah slithered off the bed. Her hair was already coming undone because of jumping on the bed and twirling around the lodge. Molly knew there was no use trying to fix her hair. She took her small bouquet of daisies in one hand and Hannah's hand in the other. "Emerson, you ready to give me away?"

Another lump bubbled up. "Yeah, Mom." Emerson smiled at her. Another few inches and she'd be taller than Molly. "Let's go get you married."

"You know, all that matters to me is that you're happy. You are happy about this right?" Molly asked.

"Yeah, I am. He's gonna be a cool step-dad. I'm totally cool with this." Emerson said. She smoothed the front of her dress and plumped the back of Hannah's, which was crinkled from sliding off the bed. The music started to play. Molly's eyes darted around the room.

"Well, that's our cue." Molly felt her palms start to sweat as she drew in a few deep breaths. "Come on girls, let's go get our guy," Molly said. Hannah squealed and stomped her feet as they made their way from the bedroom down the hall to the main lodge. "Hannah why are you stomping?"

"I'm marching, Molly. Daddy said it's the wedding march." Hannah pulled Molly's hand more as she tried to stomp harder. Molly and Emerson burst into laughter. Emerson rolled her eyes as she beamed on the other side of her mother.

As they made their way through the main lodge, Molly looked up at the antlers. She let her eyes scan the wood beams, the stone fireplace, even the old leather couches. The front desk and chair next to it were the same from her childhood. She had climbed that chair from the time she was Hannah's age. Molly had stared up at the antlers her whole life. It was part of her, part of her home, her story. The pictures on the wall were new, taken by Allie, but everything else was the same. Everything about Moose Pond Lodge was ingrained in her DNA. And now, she was marrying Zack and going to share it with him, Hannah, and Emerson. They'd be an official family from this day on. Molly wanted nothing more than to share this place with them forever. As they reached the porch, the music rolled over them. Molly leaned down to Hannah.

"Go on, sweetie. You can march to your dad. Be careful on the steps." Hannah smiled from ear to ear as she nodded. She bounced on each step and enticed giggles from everyone on either side of the aisle leading to the gazebo. Molly laughed, too. Maxine led the way next. "Okay, Em. It's our turn." Emerson walked next to Molly as they started down the porch steps. Molly thought how from the corner of her eye, Emerson could be mistaken for a full-grown woman. *It all happened in a blink* Molly thought as she walked with her daughter. She drew in another deep breath as she thought of the damage a year ago. Everything was once again so beautiful and bursting with love. Zack, as usual, worked harder than any man could to make her resort, her home, the place she loved. He repaired the cabins, porch, gazebo shingles, and redid the flower beds. Moose Pond Lodge never looked more beautiful.

Molly stepped to the edge of the porch, just past the rocking chairs. Everyone on either side of the aisle stood. She took a small step back as she forgot about that part. She glanced around at the small gathering of guests. Molly saw Zack's family, who had come to see her as part of theirs. Molly's eyes met Carl's and Martin's. The two men smiled at her simultaneously. In the year since she hired Martin to help at the lounge, he and Carl had developed a friendship that only grizzled older men seem to understand. They were a presence in each other's lives that both calmed Molly and made her remember the protection a girl feels from a father. Martin had brought her closure about her father and mother while serving as a reminder that both were more than just her parents. They were lovers, fighters, flawed, and struggling with their own demons that had nothing to do with her, and yet had everything to do with how her life had turned out. Martin winked at her as she winked at him. Winks had become a thing the two did back and forth as they exchanged smart-ass remarks about the lounge or life. Molly had come to realize over the last year that the two of them had the same sense of humor. He made her laugh every day during the busy season. Molly had to admit that if her mother had ended up with Martin, she probably would've grown to love him. He had become family, too.

She saw Maxine's husband and kids, who all gave her a quick wave. Molly's eyes then met Allie and Jonah. Allie was pregnant and showing already even though she was only four months along. Her tall, slender frame made it nearly impossible to hide. Molly flashed her a warm knowing smile as Allie placed her hand on her belly. She saw Jonah squeeze Allie's hand.

After the storm and Jonah leaving last summer, Allie spent four days wandering the resort alone crying, thinking, taking pictures, and crying some more. Once home, she and Jonah went to counseling together for a few months. Allie kept Molly in the loop about their progress working through trust issues, giving up control of each other's pain and emotions. Allie learned to rely on Jonah in a way she hadn't counted on anyone before. She discovered she could be independent, resourceful, resilient, and still be vulnerable to Jonah. He learned to love her for who she was, not who he needed her to be all the time. Jonah also learned he couldn't control everything either.

The two of them came to realize the unsettled question of where to live also played a role in their growing distance. Instead of a battle between the city and the suburbs, they decided to give Vermont a chance. After buying a small house settled on ten acres, they slowed down, especially Jonah. Allie got a job at a small paper and sold framed photographs online. She didn't have to take a subway to take pictures of trees, and Jonah didn't have to battle traffic and pent-up road rage. Jonah got a job at a marketing firm in Brattleboro but worked most days remotely. He still traveled but not like he had before. Jonah was learning the fast lane wasn't exactly the best thing for the family he hoped to have, especially if he wanted it with Allie. But Allie admitted there were still adjustment issues for Jonah, and she wasn't quite sure they'd make it work in Vermont. Then again, she told Molly, no one's marriage was ever a guarantee. Only time would tell if they'd make it work. After about six months of counseling and a major move, Allie told Jonah she was ready to try again. As they celebrated their second anniversary and impending adventure into parenthood, Molly was thrilled to have them at her wedding.

Molly glanced across the aisle at Simone. Beside Simone was the love of her life and the man she couldn't wait to bring to the lodge for a two-week retreat from their life in New York City. Plus, despite her transformation and rejection of the society life she had led with Ethan, Simone still loved getting dressed up in her finest gowns and pearls. Her hair was cut short, a fire-red pixie cut, which surprised Molly when Simone and Angel arrived a few days ago. It made her look edgy, more dangerous, than the fragile flower she was last summer. This new Simone didn't mind the dirt so much and wasn't concerned if anyone knew her boots were fresh out of the box. When they arrived days ago, Simone stepped out of the car with an air of self-confidence and determination that struck Molly like lightning. She also didn't fidget anymore.

After she left Ethan at the hospital last summer, Simone told Molly she ran straight to Angel's apartment in Brooklyn. They stayed holed up alone for weeks making love, drinking coffee and wine, eating take-out, and relishing in each other's bodies and minds. Then, Simone sold everything she had except the beach house. She and Angel bought his apartment outright and an artist's studio. Angel painted, and Simone signed up for yoga, meditation, book clubs, and even attempted a few open mic nights singing at coffee houses. Simone still wasn't sure what she wanted to do, but she was free to explore anything she wanted to each morning. She knew it wasn't realistic or financially responsible, but for the time being, she stumbled, meandered, and laughed her way through each day, each hobby, and each idea. While her family had initially shunned her, Simone told Molly that her mother had met her in the city a few times for lunch. And, Simone's mother told her she looked happy, something her mother never said before. Angel made her feel alive, giving her a reason to grow. He was her sun, moon, and rain. She beamed as any beautiful woman in love should. She also still left behind the faint scent of jasmine everywhere she went. Molly's heart leaped for her seeing the happiness burst from Simone's pores. Angel had his arm around her pale, perfectly smooth shoulder. Simone dangled her pinky from his. As Molly walked by, she saw Angel lean in and kiss her cheek. Simone had finally found her way, her home, herself, and the happiness she deserved.

As Molly passed the guests in front of white wooden chairs, she approached the gazebo. Pots of white and red miniature rose bushes lined the steps. The smell of summer in Maine filled the air. There was a hint of a cool breeze to break the humidity. Molly pulled up the corner of her dress to take a step. She looked up, and her eyes met Zack's. He smiled and extended a hand. Molly could see he was blushing. He wasn't keen on all the attention. He squeezed her hand as she made the last step and turned to face him. The pastor from town cleared his throat as Molly heard everyone take a seat. The music faded, and Emerson reached over to take her bouquet. Sunshine sat next to Hannah. His tail wagged in excitement. Molly's blood raced through her body, and her hands shook a little. Zack moved strands of her hair from her face and slid them behind her ear. His touch gave her chills. She momentarily thought of what was to come after the sun set and the guests were all gone. Emerson and Hannah were going to stay the night at Maxine's house, so they'd have the place to themselves. Molly knew she was blushing as Zack shot her a knowing look. She giggled thinking how he read her mind from the moment he pulled into Moose Pond Lodge two years ago to help her fix the place.

The vows floated above them as Molly fought tears. It wasn't so much the actual ceremony that had her choked up, but the life they were creating for themselves and their daughters. After the storm last year, Molly had the desire to put the four of them under the canopy of a giant willow tree to stay together, protected and safe forever. The ceremony was like that canopy she pictured for their little family. As she finished her vows without tears, the vision of years of growing old at Moose Pond Lodge floated into her mind. She saw the two of them on the porch in rocking chairs, dancing in the gazebo as leaves fell in fall, chasing grandkids into the lodge as the sun set.

Making snow angels with the kids and Sunshine. She could see it all, and it was perfect.

Zack leaned down to kiss her. The guests clapped and cheered. Hannah squealed above it all and the loud bang of her shoes stomping filled the gazebo. Chills ran down Molly's back. She had goosebumps on her arms as Zack pulled her in closer for a longer kiss. She smiled as he squeezed her side, something he did to her in moments of sheer bliss and ecstasy.

As the reception wound down and guests filtered out, Molly bunched the front of her dress in her hands. She sat on a rocking chair and watched Hannah run wild, with Emerson obligatorily giving chase. Zack clinked beers with the men, laughed loudly, and sent her knowing looks every chance he could. Allie sat next to her.

"How ya feeling?" Molly said.

"Good. Tired, but good. I can't believe how draining pregnancy is and it's only the beginning." She said as she rocked. She leaned her head back. "Molly, I'm so happy for you two."

"Thank you. I'm happy for you, too. I'm so relieved you guys found your way back together. You're having a family, and still made it here to come to my wedding. You're glowing."

"I wouldn't miss it for the world. This place, well, it holds a special place in my heart, and Jonah's too." Allie stopped rocking and faced her. "So, you two going away after this? A honeymoon?"

"No, we can't now. We have new guests coming tomorrow." Molly said as she stopped rocking, too. "We'll go away in the winter when things are quiet here."

"Well, being here is pretty much a honeymoon anyway." Allie said with a laugh.

"Yeah, it is." Molly realized she and Allie were sitting in the exact spot where they sat at Allie's reception two years earlier. She was rocking in that very chair when she realized she was going to stay in Maine, raise Emerson alone, run the resort that was her childhood home. It was after that realization that Zack pulled in and asked for another chance. That day, he didn't get on his knees and beg forgiveness. He didn't cry a river of tears or apologize for breaking her heart until he couldn't breathe. He didn't overwhelm her with flowers or even flowery promises. He simply walked up to her, stood in front of her and said, "I was wrong. Do you think we could try this again? I understand if you say no, but if you say yes, I think we'll both be thankful you did. We have something here, and I think if we try, it can grow into something amazing." Zack then pulled her up from that chair, took her hands and kissed her. She got the same chills at their wedding as she got two years earlier when he waltzed back into her life.

Molly inhaled the smell of cake, citronella candles, champagne bubbling idly in abandoned flutes. She heard laughter over the music and the sounds of dancing in the gazebo. She saw the lights of the gazebo come on as they did every night. She had hosted many weddings at Moose Pond Lodge the last two years. She saw a few brides and grooms party the night away as guests wandered down the trail in heels and suits, with dresses grazing the dirt trail. But this one, this day, was by far her favorite. Molly's mind suddenly went back to her childhood when she ran through the porch during other weddings. She remembered countless sunsets, nights laying on the ground watching stars poke through the black sky. She remembered sneaking beers with Maxine, playing hide and seek, and she remembered her parents. They danced on the porch some nights with guests. They laughed at the comedy shows inside on the stage. They loved under that roof, on that porch. Despite the things that went wrong in their lives and her life, it all led to this night. It all led to Zack, Molly, Hannah, and Emerson being a family at Moose Pond Lodge.

There were no guarantees they'd live happily ever after; there never were in life. But Molly smiled knowing they had a good shot at it, better than most. They had been hurt before, had seen love fade or fall apart. They had hurt each other at times. But in the end, they and their children collided on the crazy trail in front of them. They were now a family who would share Moose Pond Lodge with others. Together they'd welcome guests from all over Maine, New England, the world hopefully. Together they'd repair whatever needed fixing, clean what needed cleaning, and go out of their way to show every guest what makes the resort so special. *Always make sure they have a reason to come back to Moose Pond Lodge* her father would always say. She found herself saying that to Emerson every time a guest would put a deposit on a cabin for the next season.

While she didn't have the best of reasons to return when she did, Molly rocked in the chair and thanked God she did. Everything beautiful in her life, every source of happiness now and in the future was right in front of her. Moose Pond Lodge was her home. It was her family's home then and would be her family's home now. She watched Zack across the yard sharing a drink with Angel and Simone. Then, she glanced over at Allie's belly. Molly realized they could add to this little family if they wanted, something she had never thought about before. She watched Hannah and Emerson skip to Zack. He leaned down and kissed Hannah's head and then Emerson's. Both kids beamed as they skipped away. Yeah, Molly thought, this new family was something to nurture, something that would thrive, something that could grow. Their roots were deep and secure. Their branches intertwined, able to bend and adapt gracefully without breaking. They were strong enough to handle any storm that would come their way. They had enough sunshine in their lives, enough rain, too. Molly smiled as she rocked again. Yep, she thought, there was certainly enough room and more than enough love to go around for them to add another little one to the family at Moose Pond Lodge.

Acknowledgments

Nothing about this book, this series, was easy or effortless. While the story appeared and ingrained itself in my mind as I finished and prepared to release Moose Pond Lodge, getting it written was no easy task. However, despite being in my own way and needing the perfect environment and circumstances before I could settle in and write, it happened. The story poured from my head and onto 'paper,' so to speak. This only happens for me because of the unwavering support of my family and friends. Without my husband pushing me to do the legwork and write when possible and without feedback from friends when I'm stuck, I would never get past chapter 1 of any book or idea.

I also need to thank everyone who read The Weathering of Sea Glass and Moose Pond Lodge. Even though I had this story in my head, I didn't begin to write it until I got feedback from readers wanting to know what happened with Molly and Zack. I was hesitant to even release Moose Pond Lodge. I took a chance that no one would relate to it, get invested in the story and that no one would care if there was a sequel. Without readers encouraging me, asking for more, and showing a genuine interest and love of Moose Pond Lodge and the characters, I wouldn't have written this one. I've been moved to tears and inspired hearing from friends, family, and strangers. I've talked to book clubs, strangers at events and fairs, and have gotten feedback from online communities. Without this feedback and encouragement, these stories, characters, and towns would have remained in my head. Thank you to everyone who made me feel I could do it and that sharing these stories is worthwhile. I have many more stories in my head that I'm anxious to share. Knowing there is support out there and readers who enjoy gobbling up my little books about Maine is all the motivation and inspiration I need to keep writing and keep sharing. I can never thank readers enough for giving me and my tales a chance.

Made in the USA
Middletown, DE
22 March 2021